I0627685

Mint Flavored Trouble

Joss Miller Mysteries, Book #3

Tyora Moody

Mint Flavored Trouble
Joss Miller Mysteries, Book 3

Copyright © 2024 by Tyora Moody

Mint Flavored Trouble is a work of fiction. Names, characters, places and incidents either are products of the author's imagination or are used fictitiously. Any resemblance to actual persons, living or dead, events, or locales is entirely coincidental.

Published by
Tymm Publishing LLC
www.tymmpublishing.com

Paperback ISBN: 978-1-961437-28-9
Ebook ISBN: 978-1-961437-27-2

Cover Design: TywebbinCreations.com
Editing: Felicia Murrell

Chapter 1

Panic Attack

Tuesday, November 12 at 3:37 p.m.

I can't breathe.

My chest tightened, an invisible vise squeezed tighter with each passing second. The familiar café sounds faded away, replaced by the thunder of my own heartbeat in my ears. My vision blurred, the edges darkening as if a heavy curtain was slowly falling around me.

Panic clawed its way up my throat, threatening to escape in a scream I couldn't release. My hands trembled, and I gripped the edge of the kitchen sink. The world seemed to tilt and spin, and I felt like I was falling despite standing still.

I tried to remember what my therapist had taught me.

Breathe. Count. Ground yourself.

But I couldn't breathe.

The smell of coffee, usually so comforting, overwhelmed me.

I closed my eyes to regain control. But behind my eyelids, images flashed.

Me running.

Him pursuing.

"Joss."

Was someone saying my name?

My eyes popped open and my vision blurred. Then it cleared.

My fellow barista Briana Jones stood next to me with concern in her eyes. "Are you alright? You don't look so good."

The memory of the phone call I'd received this morning flashed through my mind. "Ms. Miller, this is the Prosecutor's Office. Chief Prosecutor Rutledge needs you to report to the Charleston County Courthouse next Monday at 10:00 a.m." The words echoed in my head, making my stomach churn.

I didn't like to burden people with my issues, so out of habit I plastered a smile on my face. "I haven't been getting a lot of sleep. Is there a crowd up front?"

Briana shook her head, her eyes searched my face. She'd known me for about two years as a co-worker, neighbor and a friend. Briana also valued privacy and gave me an understanding look. "No, it's still quiet. Fay was looking for you. She's next door in the center."

"Great. I could use a break. Are you okay working the counter?"

"Of course. And, Joss," Briana touched my arm. "You can talk to me. I know it has to be hard to be here sometimes. I don't know how you do it."

I took a deep cleansing breath. "I'm fine. Really." Yep, Briana knew me too well. So did my boss. I moved quickly toward the front of the café, skirting around the counter toward the left. Everyone wanted to keep things normal for me, and I was grateful for their thoughtfulness.

I'd hoped my memories of the attack this past summer here at the café would fade away. But they lingered like a heavy weight on my mind. Most days, I was fine. But today started out differently.

Cast all your anxiety on him, because he cares for you (1 Peter 5:7).

My next door neighbor, Eugeena Patterson-Jones shared that verse with me. I'd written it down and placed it on my bedroom mirror.

I repeated it as I left behind the scent of coffee and soft jazz to step over the threshold into the new center. In just a few months, Sugar Creek Café had merged with the neighboring building, a former craft store. Brand new double glass doors now led from inside the café to the Rebecca Montgomery Art Center. My boss Fay Everett and I had been involved in the plans for the new space, which expanded the café. Fay had tapped into her artistic side painting a colorful mural on the back wall. Not an artist myself, I had fun joining in.

It had been a kind of therapy that I needed. It was hard to think about, but over a year ago, I found the body of Maggie Nelson, the owner of the Crafty Corner. And then, this past summer, I managed to escape with my life from a crazed man. Both experiences had affected me more than I liked to admit. Through prayer and talking to my therapist, I was determined to move past my moments of PTSD.

The glass door swung shut behind me and I paused, facing the large open windows. The sun shone bright and I welcomed the warmth on my face. That and the quiet open area grounded me. Even though I'd been in this space multiple times, I still stared in amazement at the no longer recognizable former craft store.

I vaguely remembered the shelves with colorful yarn, spools of fabric and floral arrangements. Fresh paint and sawdust lingered in the air as workers continued construction inside the classrooms. In the corner were boxes of chairs and tables ready to be assembled.

I studied the tree in the center of the mural Fay had painted on the back wall. Its trunk was formed from stacks of colorful books, each spine a different hue, creating a rainbow effect that seemed to shimmer in the light. At the base of the tree, the roots spread out across the lower part of the wall. At the ends of each root were pencils, pens, and paintbrushes, stretching outward as if seeking new areas to create.

I glanced over at the framed photo of Rebecca that would greet visitors when they entered the center. She'd left a legacy of murals all across Charleston before her tragic death. The center was a fitting tribute to her memory.

"Joss! Get over here, girl!" Fay's voice cut through my thoughts.

I looked over to see my boss beckoning me, her grin wide. Fay had been all smiles the past few months. This project was special to her since she'd been friends with Rebecca. With the expansion also came the end of the dreaded development project that had threatened the café and neighboring businesses for months.

I could tell that weight had been lifted off my boss as well as the other business owners. Many people in Sugar Creek had contributed their time to the center. I'd spent time yesterday afternoon organizing books donated by the bookstore a few doors down. Books from my childhood like *Charlotte's Web* and *Roll of Thunder, Hear My Cry* were available for a new generation of readers.

As I made my way over, I couldn't help but notice the stunning woman standing next to Fay. She wore her auburn hair up in a ponytail and had high cheek bones. Her model thin shape was perfectly clad with a long gray hoodie over dark leggings. With sneakers, she stood as tall as Fay who was around 5'8. Long lashes framed doe brown eyes that warily assessed my approach.

There was something about her that seemed sad, like she was carrying a burden she couldn't quite shake. Despite her height, she stood hunched with her arms folded. I was pretty sure I'd seen her before. That wasn't unusual since most Sugar Creek residents visited the café.

"Joss, I want to introduce you to a potential volunteer," Fay said, placing a hand on the woman's shoulder. "This is Lily Hartman. She would be a great asset to helping us run music classes for kids here at the center." Fay turned to the woman. "Lily, this is Joss Miller, our resident barista extraordinaire and true crime podcaster."

Lily's eyes widened slightly at the mention of true crime. "It's a pleasure to meet you, Joss. Fay's told me so much about you and your work at the café. I love the *Cold Justice* podcast. I can't wait for the next season."

"Great to meet you too, Lily. I'm still fresh off the last season and haven't thought about what to do next."

I had a list of cases that I'd pulled together, but the first two seasons had affected my mental health. If I continued the podcast, I needed to choose wisely. I wasn't quite sure how to do that since I dealt with cold cases involving murder.

"Lily has some cool ideas." Fay clasped her hands together. "And Joss also coordinates Friday Night Jams. It was her idea for us to start doing them more than once a month."

"I enjoy working with the talent." I peered at Lily's face more closely. "You know what, I remember you from some place. Are you a singer?"

A shadow passed over Lily's face, and I immediately regretted asking.

"Yes, I sing," she said softly. "...but I have been away for a while."

An awkward quiet settled on us.

I wanted to ask why, but I felt Fay's stare before I glanced at my boss and caught her slight head shake.

Lily must have seen it too. She grimaced. "It's fine, Fay. Everybody is going to be asking questions, especially when I start showing my face more regularly."

Questions? About what?

Lily took a deep breath, her face devoid of emotion. "Most people still think I'm responsible for my husband's death."

Tuesday, November 12 at 3:52 p.m.

Lily's words hung in the air, heavy and unexpected. I opened my mouth, but before I could speak, Lily's composure crumbled. Her eyes welled up with tears, and she pressed a hand to her mouth. "I'm sorry," she choked out. "Fay, forgive me. I know you had good intentions, but I can't do this right now."

Fay reached out, but Lily turned and hurried toward the double doors.

Stunned by the women's abrupt exit, I faced Fay. "What was that about?"

Fay rubbed her temples. "I shouldn't have pushed her. She's been through so much."

My mind raced with questions. "What did she mean about people thinking she's responsible for her husband's death? Who was her husband?"

Fay held up her hands and shook her head. "Let's talk later, I've been neglecting the café long enough today. And it's just Briana in there right now."

I followed Fay through the double doors, my mind on something other than my earlier anxiety attack. Sure enough, the café had filled up and Briana looked at us with relief as we returned behind the counter.

We worked together to take care of the patrons until I flipped the sign on the door to Closed. I'd almost forgotten about Lily until Briana asked, "What were you and Fay talking to Lily Hartman about? I haven't seen her in ages."

I glanced over at Briana as I replenished the sugar packets on the condiment counter. "You know her?"

"Yeah. I know it's been awhile, but I'm surprised you don't remember her. She had changed her hair, and she wasn't wearing makeup. She used to come to Friday Night Jams. In fact, she sang with *Indigo Soul* before I stepped in. Lily has always been good at reinventing herself, I heard."

I liked to call Briana our Beyoncé of Sugar Creek. When she wasn't working at the café, she was on the road singing solo or with a local favorite, the rhythm and blues band, *Indigo Soul*.

I slapped my hand over my forehead. "That's where I remembered her from. Wow, that was a few years ago, but I knew there was something about her that looked familiar. What happened? She kind of mentioned her husband before she hightailed it out of here."

Briana tilted her head. "*That's* what happened, girl. Actually, she stopped with the band when they got married. Let's just say there was some drama with a certain band member. Anyhow, she and her husband had only been married about a year when he died."

I held my hand over my chest. "Oh my! They were still newlyweds. I can't imagine. Who was her husband?"

Briana eyed me. "C'mon, Joss. You're the queen of true crime. I know you remember the choir director who was found dead on Christmas Eve last year?"

My eyes widened as the pieces clicked into place. "Vince Hartman? Lily is Vince Hartman's widow?"

Fay's voice pierced our conversation. "What are you two talking about?"

We were gossiping. I exchanged glances with Briana, suddenly feeling sheepish. I lifted my shoulders. "Briana was telling me about Lily. I'm sorry. I know she's your friend, but she left after dropping that bomb statement. And I was curious."

Fay leaned against the counter and crossed her arms. "I know, and I left you hanging. It was a terrible situation. Folks loved Vince. He was easy on the eyes and had a voice that could take you into worship. When he died... Well, people wanted someone to blame. Lily became the target of a lot of ugly speculation."

I felt a familiar tug in my gut. "But she was never charged, right? I remember the case was never solved."

"No charges," Fay confirmed. "But accusations can be as damaging as a conviction. Lily has been suffering from depression. Who can blame her? Her mother was the music teacher back when I used to teach art. She reached out to me, desperate to get Lily back into the land of the living."

Briana shook her head. "Don't you think her being at the center will stir up a lot of old gossip?"

Fay's expression hardened. "Lily deserves a chance to rebuild her life. She's an incredible singer and an accomplished pianist. The kids will be lucky to learn from her."

Briana turned away as if she'd been scolded. "I hope it turns out good for everyone involved. I'm going to grab my stuff."

After Briana walked away, I turned to Fay. "Maybe if someone tried to clear Lily's name, she could get her life back too."

"Joss," Fay warned. "I know that look. Whatever you're thinking, be careful."

I met Fay's gaze, seeing the concern there. "Don't worry. I haven't been thinking about the podcast."

Fay's eyes softened. "How are you doing, Joss? You know you and Lily have a lot in common."

I eyed my boss. "What's that?"

Fay reached out and touched my arm. "You both hide your pain. Or you think you're hiding it, but it's all over your face."

I stepped away from Fay's touch. "I'm not in pain. Everything is fine with me."

Fay sighed, "That's not what I meant—"

Before Fay could finish her words, a loud knock echoed from the front of the café.

We both spun around to see who was at the café door after closing.

Chapter 2
Anxiety Reigns

Tuesday, November 12 at 6:27 p.m.

Briana swept past us with a puzzled expression. "What's wrong with y'all? It's just Joss's man coming to pick her up. I was just about to ask you if you needed a ride home." Briana's eyes narrowed, "Looks like you have no intentions of going home."

I laughed while my heartbeat slowed. "He's going to take me to look at cars tomorrow. I'm going to take your advice and visit Carlson Auto. I really hate to give up my ole' girl, but she's no longer trustworthy."

My boss pouted. "Girl, life ain't the same once you get a car note. That's good Andre is going with you. You're gonna need someone who can finagle the price. I'm glad Joe came with me."

Fay purchased a car a month ago. My boss opted for a brand new Toyota Camry. I received a decent enough paycheck, but I planned on perusing the used car lot.

Briana opened the door to let in Andre. "Hey, detective."

Detective Andre Baez smiled at Briana. "Hey, Briana. Good to see you. You've been on the road for a while."

Briana grinned. "Yes, the band had a lot of gigs up and down the east coast the past few months. I'm hoping with the holidays coming up, we can slow down a bit. It's good to not be sleeping in hotels for a change." Briana waved, "I'm heading home to put my feet up. Good night, y'all."

"Andre, I'll be right there." I sprinted to the back to grab my bag from my locker. But then I stopped and glanced at the back door. Of course it was shut tight and Briana had taken the trash out earlier. Still I stared as if I expected the door to be open.

Like it was that night a few months ago when someone had broken in and attacked me, I shivered as the memory rolled through me like a sharp breeze.

I need to get out of here.

My fingers trembled as I fumbled with the locker latch. I tried to slow my breathing while I reached for my bag. It was heavy with a ton of items I thought I might need for the overnight stay with Andre. Somehow the weight grounded me as I swung the bag onto my shoulder.

By the time I returned to the front of the café, Andre was standing at the counter talking to Fay. They both turned to look at me with concern in their eyes. I groaned inwardly, knowing I had probably been the subject of their conversation. I had no doubt Andre had asked Fay about me or, knowing my boss, she might've volunteered information. Their concern both comforted and bothered me.

I smiled. "Fay, you sure you don't need my help tomorrow?"

Fay waved me away. "I'll be fine. Wednesdays are your usual day off. I hope you all find something. Having decent transportation is a must."

I hooked my arm into Andre's and giggled. "I agree, but having a handsome chauffeur doesn't hurt either."

Andre grinned down at me. "You know I'm here for whatever you need, babe."

My cheeks grew warm and I couldn't help but stare into his eyes.

"Y'all need to go cause it looks like you need a room." Fay's sharp voice interrupted my being mesmerized by the man I'd known over a year now.

Not even the least bit embarrassed, I followed Andre out to his car. Raised by a strict mama and growing up with three sisters, Andre was a true gentleman. Whenever he opened doors for me, it never failed to make me feel special.

As I settled into the passenger seat, the familiar scent of his car – a mix of leather and his cologne – enveloped me. I felt calm and at ease as Andre slid into the driver's seat. I always thought guys leaned back too far in the driver's seat. But Andre made it look good – and sexy as he gripped the steering wheel and started the engine. It must be time for my monthly friend to visit. My emotions were all over the place today.

A familiar song filled the car as Andre coasted out of the parking lot. I hadn't realized how much my feet hurt until my body melted into the bucket seat. Being on my feet all day left me feeling tired, but lately I felt extra exhausted. I knew it was a lack of sleep. The dreams were back, not that they ever really left. Thoughts crowded my mind, and I didn't hear Andre talking to me.

I felt him peering at me and jerked. The concern in his brown eyes was so palpable, my cheeks felt flushed. Thankfully, the dashboard lights didn't illuminate the inside of the car well. "Sorry, I'm pretty tired. What did you say?"

Andre braked for a red light before studying me. "I was asking about food. What do you want to eat tonight?"

"Oh," I said, feeling ashamed. Andre probably had a hard day at work too. Being a homicide detective wasn't easy, and he'd been using his free time to help me. I blew out a breath. "Whatever you want is fine with me."

Andre cocked an eyebrow. "Okay. This sounds like a test."

I laughed and patted his arm. "I promise it's not a test. I trust you." And I did. We'd been dating long enough that Andre knew what I liked. He hadn't steered me wrong so far. And I was hungry. I'd downed too much coffee and not enough nourishing foods.

In the comfortable silence, I nodded off. Andre was the first man I'd been with where quiet moments didn't feel awkward. I liked that. I didn't have to fill the silence; I could sit with him for long stretches of time enjoying his company.

My lids lazily slid open and a warmth crept up my chest when I saw the restaurant Andre had selected. "You did good."

"I figured I couldn't go wrong with Chinese."

It occurred to me that I still had on my Sugar Creek Café uniform. I sat up looking at the other cars in the parking lot. "Are we going to eat inside?"

Andre pulled out his phone. "We can order on the app and pick up the food."

I lifted my finger. "That sounds like a plan."

I watched as he pressed a familiar app. After a few moments of him arched over the phone in concentration, he turned and looked at me. "Ordered. I'll wait ten minutes before I go in to pick it up."

"Oh, so it's a surprise." I teased.

He gave me a lopsided grin. "You did say you trusted me. I ordered your usual."

I crossed my arms and pretended to frown. "I didn't realize I was so predictable."

He shook his head. "Not at all. In fact, there are plenty of things I don't know about you. Like what's bothering you. Is everything okay?"

Wow, he does know me too well.

I hesitated for a moment, debating what to share. I don't know why, but I opted to remove myself as the topic for discussion and instead, I blabbered. "I met Lily Hartman today."

Andre's eyebrows shot up. "Vince Hartman's widow?"

And just like that I'd wiggled myself right back into the conversation. "Yeah. Do you know the case?"

He nodded, "I know the detectives on the case. It appeared to be a one car accident."

I interrupted, "But something weird came up?"

Andre lifted an eyebrow. "I see you're interested, but yeah. There were skid marks and from further examination of Mr. Hartman's vehicle, it had been hit."

"So someone ran him off the road?"

"That's the consensus." Andre replied. "So I take it Mrs. Hartman doesn't visit the café regularly since she's a sudden interest."

"She used to. Even participated in Friday Night Jams. According to Fay, she's been staying to herself. Apparently, Lily's mother talked to Fay about getting her involved in the center. I don't think she's ready though. It sounds like she's self-conscious about people blaming her for her husband's death."

Andre glanced at me. "As you know, when a death appears to be foul play, they will look at the spouse. In this case, there was also an ex-wife too."

I lifted my eyebrow. "Really? I didn't know that. That explains why they'd only been married about a year. So Lily was the second wife."

TYORA MOODY

He nodded. "That's what I've been told. If the divorce wasn't amicable and the ex-wife felt she'd been tossed aside for a younger woman..."

I sat up in the seat. "Then the ex-wife could be a suspect. Did they check her out?"

Andre nodded. "I'm sure they did. Is there a reason why you're interested in the Vince Hartman case?"

I shook my head. "I'm curious. I'd heard about it, but I guess I didn't really pay attention to it. Around this time last year, I was still getting over the aftereffects of my first podcast season."

Andre reached for my hand. "And you're still probably feeling overwhelmed from the last one. Look, I know you, Joss Miller. Once you start asking questions, your interest will only grow. I'm about to head in to grab our order."

I turned up my nose as I watched him slide out of the car and head toward the restaurant. I wanted to be annoyed. Andre had a way of subtly pushing his concerns. Without explicitly saying so, he was warning me that I shouldn't show too much interest. I placed my head back against the headrest knowing he was right. When I started digging into a true crime, the discovery of truth had been coming back to bite me.

Andre returned quickly and handed me the brown bag. The tangy, aromatic scents wafting from the bag comforted my senses until my mind shifted back to Lily and her deceased husband. As Andre drove away, I wondered. How far was I intending to dive into my new interest?

Tuesday, November 12 at 7:24 p.m.

Andre pulled into his driveway. We tried not to make overnight stays a habit, but it would be easier to head to the dealership in the morning if I spent the night at his place. It worried me sometimes that we were at this weird crossroads in our relationship.

In my early twenties, I'd moved in with my past boyfriends despite my mom's objections to my "shacking." Once I had to move out due to the demise of a relationship, Clarice Miller had no problem telling her only daughter, 'I told you so.'

I would never admit to her that I often thought I was in love but really had been caught up in the romance and passion. When I moved in with my biological grandmother two years ago, I chose not to date for a long time. Something about entering my late twenties made me more cautious about moving forward intimately with a man. So far, Andre honored the celibacy rules between us, but that wasn't always easy.

Especially when we were alone.

The first time I saw him with his shirt off, I had to pray hard. And there was a time or two, okay probably a lot more, when Andre's hands eased under my shirt, unclasping my bra. Neither of us were virgins, so we had lots of awkward moments. I really didn't know how long we could keep it up. And maybe in some ways, I hadn't expected us to be together this long either.

Until something changed, like something more permanent, I would see where God led us.

Andre's bachelor pad was clean and comfortable. The same leather he liked in his car was also featured throughout his living room. The soft leather sectional was easy to re-arrange for watching television and relaxing. I pulled off my shoes and left them by the door. The open concept floorplan had wall-to-wall plush beige carpeting in the living room. I shuffled across the area in my socks until I reached the oak wood flooring that covered the rest of the space into the large kitchen.

After consuming a few meals over at his place, I soon realized why Andre had such a large kitchen. He loved to cook and would often do so after a long day at work. He'd told me slicing vegetables or hearing the sizzle of meat in a skillet eased the tension from his body. He must have had an extraordinarily hard day to suggest takeout.

I placed the bag on the oblong dining table while Andre grabbed some plates. "I have some freshly brewed iced tea."

"That sounds great." I pulled the Styrofoam containers out of the bag. "Wow, they always fill these up so much. You can eat for days out of this."

He filled glasses with ice from his ice maker. Andre managed to hold the plates, two glasses and the pitcher of iced tea.

"Let me help you with that." We both chuckled as I took the pitcher from his hand and set it on the table.

Andre spun around. "We need utensils."

I grabbed his arm. "We will be fine with the plastic ones. Sit down. I want to hear about your day."

He smiled at me and stared into my eyes. The warmth in his gaze made me blush. The one thing I always felt with this man was safe. "You're right, let's eat. And you don't want to hear about my day. "

I pulled out a seat and sat down. "Were you called to a crime scene today?"

He nodded instead of answering. I watched as he piled fried rice onto his plate. Andre carefully shared his work with me sometimes, but most of the time he kept it to himself.

Knowing that I had my own issues I'd rather not discuss, I fixed my plate. We ate in silence with only the sounds of a dog barking a few yards down. I would miss my feline roommate tonight. My grandmother had three cats and the female cat of the house, Minnie, often kept me company.

"Have you given anymore thought to getting a dog?"

He looked up at me, surprised. "Where did that come from?"

"Hearing the dog barking outside."

He nodded. "That would be one of Mr. Winters' dogs. He actually works at the animal shelter and all three of his dogs are rescues."

"Three?" I listened more carefully. "Yeah, I can hear distinctive barks."

Andre frowned, "I would love to have a dog. I have plenty of yard space in the back for one, but my hours are crazy. I figured one day, you know, when I have a family, then I'll get a dog."

I croaked, "Family. Yeah, that makes sense." We'd tossed the subject around. I knew both of us liked kids and animals. Those were green flags. But marriage...

I paused, confused. Andre was still talking, but I had drifted. "Did you say something about Thanksgiving? You're going to Charlotte to be with your family, right?"

Andre shook his head. "No, I was saying Mama and my sisters wanted to come here this year instead and..." he trailed off, looking slightly sheepish. "Well, they figured it would be easier for all of them to meet you here in Charleston."

"Meet me?" My voice came out higher than I intended.

Andre quickly added, "Hey, no pressure, Joss. They're excited, that's all. I'm the only male in the family, so there is no such thing as a private life where my sisters are concerned."

I tried to smile, but anxiety had already crept in. I'd briefly met Andre's mom and one sister. I knew two of his more vocal sisters would come prepared to interrogate me. At least that's what Andre teased all the time.

After we finished dinner and I'd cleaned up the table, Andre headed upstairs to his bedroom to take a shower. I headed toward the hallway bath with my overnight bag. Since I spent the night on occasion, and Andre was opening his home for family to come visit, he'd invested in furnishing the other two bedrooms in his townhome. The room across from the hall bath served as part workout room and part bedroom. After washing up and fixing my hair for the night, I headed down the hallway to the other bedroom. I'd helped Andre decorate this bedroom. Out of all the rooms in the house, it had more of a feminine touch. I imagined his mother or sisters, whoever was coming up for Thanksgiving, would be pleased with the progress on Andre's bachelor pad.

Just as I placed the silk bonnet over my hair, there was a knock at the door. I still had on my fluffy pink robe, so I felt I was presentable enough. "Come in."

Andre stood in the doorway dressed in a white t-shirt and gray lounge pants. "You mind if we talk a minute?"

"Sure." I sat down on the bed and while I shouldn't have, I invited him to sit next to me. He came over and took my hand, his thumb tracing gentle circles on my skin. "How are you really doing? And don't say 'fine.' I know you better than that."

"Do I look that bad?"

He chuckled. "I can tell something is worrying you. Have you been sleeping?"

Knots curled in my stomach and I was pretty sure they weren't from dinner. I took a breath. "I'm f... managing. The doctor gave me some medicine that helps me sleep." I closed my eyes, not realizing a tidal wave of tears were ready to flow. "It stopped the nightmares for a while, but with the grand jury coming up..."

Andre squeezed my hand. "You're going to be fine. You've met Rutledge. He's a really good prosecutor and he knows how to win cases. Caleb Davenport is going to stay behind bars a long time."

I knew Andre was right. I'd met Charleston's Chief Prosecutor Michael Rutledge on at least two occasions. He was a handsome white man with graying hair around the sides. Rutledge also was the father of three daughters, all whose pictures sat on his desk. He was appalled and sympathetic to what I'd gone through. I had no doubt he would put Caleb away where he belonged. I just wanted to put it behind me forever.

I opened my eyes, appreciating that Andre held my hand. I leaned closer into him relishing his warm body next to mine.

He placed his arm around me pulling me close. "Would it help if I walk you through what to expect?"

I nodded, "Yeah. Rutledge tried to explain it to me, but it all feels daunting. I've never been through something like this before. Never even been selected for a jury."

Andre shook with laughter. "Being on a jury is definitely an experience." He straightened, growing more serious. Okay, first off, remember that this isn't a trial. The grand jury's job is to decide if there's enough evidence to bring formal charges against Caleb," he explained. "We already know the evidence is pretty solid."

"So, I won't have to face him, right?" My voice sounded small, like I'd reverted back to a much younger version of myself.

Andre shook his head. "No, Caleb won't be there. It will be you, the jurors, the prosecutor, and maybe a court reporter. No judge, no defense attorney."

I let out a breath I didn't know I was holding.

Andre continued, his hand rubbing up and down my arm. "The prosecutor will ask you questions about what happened that night at the café. Just tell the truth, exactly as you remember it. And that's all there is to it."

A jolt seized my chest and I stiffened. "But what if I can't remember everything?" The memories of that night were sometimes a blur of terror and adrenaline.

I don't want to remember.

"That's okay," Andre reassured me. "Just be honest about what you do remember. If you're not sure about something, it's fine to say so. Just be honest. The jurors need to understand what happened to you."

"How long will it take?" I asked, dreading the thought of reliving that night in front of strangers.

"It varies, but probably no more than an hour or two." He patted my shoulders. "You should probably get to bed. I know you're tired. If you need me, I will be right upstairs."

I lifted my face to him and he bent to kiss me. It was a long, slow kiss that had me hot and bothered under the fluffy robe. We parted and stared into each other's eyes. I wanted to ask him to stay or if maybe I could go upstairs with him.

I had a feeling he was thinking the same so he pulled back and stood from the bed. Andre cleared his throat. "Your testimony is crucial in making sure Caleb faces justice, not only for attacking you, but possibly for Rebecca too."

"Thanks." I managed a weak smile. "Good night, Andre."

His eyes lingered on me awhile longer. "Good night, babe."

Grateful that he closed the door before he saw my face glow in the dark. My cheeks, as well as other parts, were awfully warm.

I turned the covers back and then bent down beside the bed to pray. My prayer had been consistent. *Lord, help me to put that night behind me and keep going on with my life.* I climbed under the covers and smiled. God had already answered one long-time prayer.

I'd fallen in love with the right man.

Chapter 3
Finding Trouble

Wednesday, November 13 at 10:00 a.m.

I fidgeted in the passenger seat as Andre pulled into the parking lot of Carlson Auto. My trusty Honda Civic had finally let me down. I liked to refer to her as "my girl." She'd been with me over ten years and had been a part of major life changes. My stomach did cartwheels as I faced the sea of shiny vehicles sparkling in the morning sun. It felt weird replacing her even though she had too many things wrong with her to fix.

Would I drive off the lot with a replacement today?

Thank goodness Andre took some time off work to accompany me. I considered myself an independent woman, but big purchases like this brought back memories of the men in my life. My father had helped with my first car.

The second year I had my first car, I'd smacked the back of a Yukon at a traffic light. I broke down in tears in front of a stranger and state patrolman. The tears were for far more than the accident. It'd only been a few months since my dad died and I'd just totaled the car. I felt like I let down the man who'd patiently taught me to drive. If he were alive, he would have been more concerned about my wellbeing than my mistake.

My brother helped me file the insurance claim and took me to buy the Honda Civic. Now he had moved out of the state and I rarely saw him.

"Remind me again why we're here?" Andre's voice broke into my trip down memory lane.

I grinned at him. "Briana recommended this place. She said they had great deals and the sales staff was super friendly. Might as well check it out, right?"

A small smile played on his lips. "Well, let's see if we can find the car of your dreams."

I laughed. We were about to look at used cars, which I hoped I could afford. There was a luxury in not having a car payment and I wasn't looking forward to the loss of funds each month.

As we stepped out of the car, a man with a similar complexion to Andre moved into my peripheral vision. Either he'd been standing in front of the dealership in the shadows or had just walked out. I wondered where I'd seen him before. His face looked familiar, but the short dreadlocks and beard were throwing me off.

There was something about his eyes.

"Hey folks, can I help you?" He stepped toward us and looked at me for a few seconds, like he was trying to figure out where he'd seen me too. My face was a familiar fixture at Sugar Creek Café. I worked there several days a week.

Andre answered, "We're just looking for now. Where are the used cars?"

The man gave Andre the customary head nod that men liked to exchange. "Sure, if you head over to the right, we have plenty for you to check out. If you need anything, I'm KJ."

Andre returned the head nod. "Thanks, man. Appreciate it."

KJ stepped back into the shadows of the building.

"That was nice, he's letting us look."

Andre glanced back. "I'm sure he's keeping an eye on us. As soon as it looks like you've set your mind on a car, he'll be right beside us ready to make the sale."

We browsed down a row, and I wrinkled my nose at a bright yellow Volkswagen Beetle. "Too conspicuous."

Andre pointed to a sleek red sports car. "What about that one?"

"On a barista's salary?" I laughed. "Besides, I'd probably scrape the bottom on every speed bump in Charleston."

Andre laughed. "You are a bit hard on a car, babe."

"Hey." I smacked his arm. "I had my girl for ten years."

We passed a Civic that reminded me of my girl, and I quickly moved past it. I wanted to replace my car with something totally new.

We turned down another row, and a tall broad-shouldered man with dark skin and an easy smile approached us from behind. It felt like he appeared out of nowhere. I hadn't even heard his footsteps.

His approach may have been quiet, but his voice boomed. "Welcome to Carlson Auto! I'm Terrell. How can I help you folks today?"

Where was the other salesman? KJ.

Andre answered before I could comment. "KJ is helping us out."

Terrell waved his hands as if it wasn't a big deal. "Yeah, he's okay with me taking this one."

I exchanged a look with Andre, wondering if KJ actually said that. Could have been more like snooze you lose.

Terrell continued, his brown eyes twinkling in the sunlight. "We have the best selection in Charleston. I see you're in the used car section. Any particular make or model you're interested in?"

Ugh. Unlike KJ, who was polite, this guy was a total salesman. I hadn't thought about a make or model. I figured I would lay eyes on the car that was for me. I frowned and confessed, "My last car was a Honda. So, maybe another Honda or possibly a Toyota."

Terrell laughed heartily, "Both are good choices. We have a great selection of both."

Since it looked like we weren't getting rid of Terrell, we let him guide us up and down several rows. Andre did more chatting with the salesman than me. The guy probably figured Andre was doing the purchasing. Not! I stopped as my eyes fell on a red Toyota RAV4. I knew it was an older model, but I had heard those were the best small crossover vehicles, and it was similar in hue to my red Civic.

But did I have the budget for it?

Terrell walked up to me. A little too close for my comfort, so I stepped back bumping into Andre. He slipped his arm around my waist as if protecting me.

Terrell grinned, "I see you've found one that you like. We have a great sale going on right now. We can knock at least $500 off this sticker price."

$500. That sounded like a lot, but when I looked at the pricing, it still inched up close to $20,000. I blew out a breath. Cars weren't this expensive ten years ago. "Let me keep looking around. I will come back to this one."

Terrell gave me a toothy grin. "Okay. Let me know when you want to test drive this baby."

Andre and I strolled a bit farther away. Terrell stayed a considerable distance behind. He wasn't breathing down our throats, but, without turning around, I was aware he was back there.

I stated in a low voice. "He's sticking to us like superglue."

Andre chuckled. "These guys make their bread and butter from the sale. He doesn't want to lose your sale today. I have to admit I liked the other guy's demeanor better."

Me too!

We walked a full circle around the used car section and somehow managed to stand back in front of the RAV4. I turned to Terrell, who still trailed behind us. He was on his phone frowning at something on the screen.

Andre rubbed my shoulder. "Looks like this is the one you want."

"I certainly have been pulled toward it. I guess I will know better after we test drive it."

"I'll get the keys."

I almost jumped out of my skin at the salesman's booming voice. I turned and caught him sprinting back inside.

Andre commented, "You're kind of jumpy today. Did you get any sleep?"

I nodded. "I did. I slept well."

Andre narrowed his eyes but didn't have a chance to ask me anything else. Terrell returned with the keys and opened the driver's side door. I climbed in, and Andre entered the back and slid over behind the passenger seat. I glanced back at him and smiled.

He winked at me. "This is nice. Looks good on the inside, but we will want to look under the hood too."

Terrell opened the passenger door and fit his large girth into the seat. "Did I hear you want to look under the hood?"

Andre sat back. "Yeah, we can do that after Joss takes us for a spin."

"Sounds good." Terrell looked at me. "Are you ready?"

"Yes," I responded. My voice sounded like a squeak. I swallowed, feeling a bit apprehensive. I wasn't sure if it was my first time driving this car or Terrell looming large and opposing in the passenger's seat that fueled my nerves.

I took a right out of the dealership and blended with the traffic. I felt pretty comfortable, like I'd been driving the car all my life. I veered off the exit ramp toward I-26 where the traffic was much heavier. By the time I headed back to the dealership, I was sold.

"You can pull in here." Terrell guided me to the back of the lot.

I rubbed the steering wheel before climbing out.

"What did you think?" Andre asked, already waiting for me as I stepped out of the car.

I looked up from examining the car's shiny metallic red exterior. "I loved it. It felt so natural, like it's already mine. I hope that's not a bad thing."

Andre lifted an eyebrow. "How many miles is on this?"

Terrell answered, "It's got 17,456 miles. The previous owner was an older lady and rarely used it except for doctor's appointments." He pulled the lever for the hood and then lifted it. "Take a look. I promise you it's in good condition."

Andre nodded as he scanned the inner workings under the hood. He righted himself and stepped back. "If you can provide the official paperwork to view that would be great."

"Of course. Sounds like this is the one. If you want, we can head inside to my office."

Andre placed his hands on the small of my back and guided me behind Terrell into the dealership. Inside his cubicle, Terrell explained their financing and maintenance plans which all seemed to go over my head a bit. I filled out the paperwork and handed it to him.

"Joss. Joss Miller. That name sounds familiar. Do you have a podcast?"

I grinned, I expected my local celebrity status might come up. Maybe I could get another discount. "Yes, I produce the *Cold Justice* podcast."

He nodded. "We have a few fans. Sometimes we play a podcast on the sound system instead of music."

"That's pretty cool."

My eyes caught sight of Terrell's nameplate. The name "Hartman" jumped out at me and a connection clicked in my mind. "Hartman... Any relation to Lily Hartman?"

Terrell's easy smile vanished and his expression turned cold.

"I have nothing in common with *that* woman."

The hairs on my arm rose and the air seemed to shift around us.

Wednesday, November 13 at 11:02 a.m.

Not sure what to say or do, I sought direction from Andre. My normally calm and cool boyfriend had deep frown lines in his forehead. An indication that he wasn't pleased with Terrell's tone either. "She didn't mean anything by her question."

I nodded. "Andre's right. I'm sorry, I didn't mean to offend you, Terrell. I met Lily the other day and saw your last name—"

Terrell slammed the pen in his hand onto the desk, his friendly salesman pitch gone. "Vince was my brother," his voice clipped.

Inwardly, I grimaced at my mistake. "I didn't know."

It felt like Terrell loomed over me even though he was sitting down. Through clenched jaws, he demanded, "What were you talking to her about?"

Stunned, I looked at Andre who glared back at the man. "Joss, let's go. This is entirely unprofessional." He stood. "We should head somewhere else."

At a loss for words, I stood, feeling sick to my stomach.

How could this go wrong? I really liked that car.

"Is there a problem?" A man's voice came from behind.

I spun to find a caramel toned man dressed impeccably in a crisp white shirt and dark gray slacks. He couldn't have been older than Andre, but he wore circular spectacles at the end of his nose like a much older man.

With his hand cupped around my elbow, Andre shook his head, "We were just leaving."

The man's sharp brown eyes swept briefly behind us before his gaze landed on me. He held out his hand toward me. "I'm Grant Carlson. Now I saw *you* come back from the test drive and I've been doing this long enough to know you loved *that* car. Won't you come to my office and we can discuss terms?"

I may have sighed out loud. I really didn't want to leave without *that* car. Without saying a word, I stared at Andre, silently pleading. I knew my eyes were on the verge of tears. I wasn't afraid. Somehow, I felt like I'd messed up. I wanted that few minutes back when I hadn't uttered a word.

We never spoke about it, but I wasn't the only one affected by my attack this past summer. My knight in shining armor arrived right on time, and I suspected Andre had been on edge ever since. Terrell had no idea my overprotective boyfriend he was insulting was one of Charleston Police Department's finest.

Andre met my gaze and I watched his face soften. He blew out a breath and shrugged his shoulders. "Sure, this was all a misunderstanding."

Grant smiled, "Yes, it was." He turned, "Cindy, can you show this lovely young couple to my office?"

A heavyset woman with a short salt and pepper bob stood from behind the large reception desk. She stepped around the desk, wearing a knit dress that fit her full figure, and her face held a bright smile. Almost too bright and friendly. I imagine she and others were embarrassed, or even horrified, by Terrell's outburst.

As she drew closer, despite her heavy makeup I caught a resemblance in her eyes and complexion to Mr. Carlson. I wondered if Carlson Auto was a family business.

"Follow me." She strutted with purpose down a hallway lined with closed office doors rather than cubicles.

Before we started off behind the woman, I looked back to find Terrell with his head in his hands. A co-worker had walked over to talk to him. It was KJ, the salesman who approached us first when we arrived. I hoped he didn't light into Terrell for snatching his sale. Now I felt like we would have been in better hands with KJ as our salesperson.

Still, I felt bad for Terrell. I could've kicked myself for being so thoughtless. Lily married into the Hartmans. This man had lost a brother this time last year. Though his reaction totally caught me off guard, it raised my curiosity too. If that was the kind of reaction she'd received from her deceased husband's family, there was no wonder why Lily had been hiding away.

Grant's office was at the end of the hall, and by the size of it, he had to be the boss. I almost forgot about what happened when we stepped inside the sleek, modern interior. One wall of the office was a floor-to-ceiling glass pane that looked out onto the showroom, where the latest luxury car models gleamed under spotlights. The opposite wall featured giant posters of all types of cars, mainly sports cars.

Carlson Auto was one of the largest car dealerships in Sugar Creek. It catered to two types of car buyers. Those who could afford the finest of cars. And the lowly worker like me, looking for a vehicle that fit her budget.

Cindy swept her hand across a set of chairs in front of a massive desk. "You two can have a seat. Can I get you anything? Coffee, water, soda?"

Andre declined. "I'm good. Thank you."

"I'll take some water," I said. My throat had grown dry. I crossed over to the chair closest to the wall and perched on the edge.

"Sure thing, hon." Cindy walked over to a small refrigerator in the corner of the office and pulled out a bottled water. "Here you go. Grant will be with you in a second. I'm so sorry about Terrell. I heard what happened." She glanced over her shoulder and lowered her voice, "All of us did."

I protested. "I didn't know."

Cindy held out her hand as if she was soothing a child. "Of course you didn't, hon. You're here buying a car. The thing is... Vince, that's Terrell's brother, he passed away last year. Right on Christmas Eve."

My parched throat felt relieved as I gulped the ice cold water. I was no stranger to missing loved ones during the holidays, but Terrell's strong reaction to me mentioning his brother's wife still disturbed me. Did he hate the woman that much? And if so, why?

Grant stepped inside the office, holding papers. "Thank you, Cindy."

"No problem, boss man." On the way out, the woman flashed a big smile. "I hope you get the car you want. Grant's going to take good care of you." When she closed the door behind her, the noise and conversations from outside the office could no longer be heard.

Grant sat behind his desk and placed the papers in front of him. Across from us, he appeared friendly, but also like the man in charge. "First, I'm sorry about that. I hope Terrell's emotional outburst won't reflect on Carlson Auto."

"Of course not." I started. "Um, the mistake was mine."

Andre shook his head. "Joss, you couldn't have known that."

Grant nodded, "Agreed. And no worries." He reached for the paperwork on his desk. "Now, I see you're interested in purchasing the pearl ruby Toyota RAV4. Such a beautiful color."

The smile I'd had before the fumble returned. "Yes, I really loved driving it. I think it fits me." I glanced over at Andre who still looked a bit perturbed.

He caught my look and the wrinkles across his forehead smoothed. "You did look good in it."

Grant stated, "Well, let's get this baby ready for you to take home. I believe I can work out a better deal for you."

I smiled, feeling the tension completely leave my body. "That sounds like a plan."

While Andre wasn't a lawyer, he actually read the paperwork, which I appreciated. Several pieces of paper received my signature, and then Grant handed me two key fobs.

"I hope you enjoy your new ride. You will get free maintenance for a year. If you have any problems, my card is in here." Grant passed a larger white envelope with Carlson Auto imprinted on the front.

"Thank you. I appreciate everything."

As Andre and I left the office, I couldn't help but take a look at Terrell's cubicle. He wasn't there. For a second, I felt apprehensive. Hopefully, the salesman hadn't gotten into serious trouble.

Chapter 4

The Fallout

Thursday, November 14 at 2:30 p.m.

I wiped down the tables after the lunch crowd subsided. Like a kid with a new toy, every chance I got, I was at the window peering across the street. My new-to-me bright red ... no that's ruby pearl ...car sparkled in the parking lot.

"Are you daydreaming, Joss?" A familiar voice made me burst out laughing.

Eleanor, our resident author, chuckled from the booth that was unofficially her office space.

"Just admiring my new ride. At least until the first car payment is due."

"Well, that's something to smile about. Let me guess, it's that bright red one." Eleanor teased.

I frowned. "How did you know?"

With a twinkle in her eye, Eleanor cupped her hands over her mouth. "I followed a few clues."

I slapped my hand over my forehead and shook with laughter. "Of course, my last car was red. I guess I'm kind of predictable. As a mystery writer, I'm sure you write better clues."

Eleanor shook her finger. "Oh, sometimes clues are very obvious, and sometimes they're just hidden in plain sight."

"Speaking of clues, did you talk to Fay about doing the book signing for *The Last Brushstroke* in the art center? I think it would be really cool."

Eleanor leaned back in the booth. "Yes, she agreed it would be a good idea. I appreciate you suggesting it."

Like writers tend to do, Eleanor merged real life headlines into her cozy mysteries. The shrewdest of readers, like myself, recognized real people within the characters and plots. In *The Last Brushstroke*, Eleanor's heroine bore a striking resemblance to Rebecca Montgomery, the slain artist. Eleanor gifted me with an advanced copy a few weeks ago. I'd read most of her books and while the story felt close, it was also vastly different. The victim met a similar fate. But the main character, an older woman I long suspected to be the author herself, managed to end on a happier note.

"It seemed fitting since Rebecca was your inspiration."

Eleanor's eyes appeared sad for a moment. "Yes, it was my way of shedding some light on her tragedy." She looked at me. "But you really brought her justice. How are you doing?"

"I'm good. Well, as good as I can be." I sighed. Eleanor was one of those people I found myself spilling my guts to. I stepped closer to her table and lowered my voice. "I have to testify at the grand jury next Monday."

Eleanor reached out and touched my arm. "Oh no. That must have you pretty anxious. You know you won't have to see him."

My body shivered. "No, I just need to tell strangers how he came after me."

Eleanor patted my hand. "You will do fine. I'm glad you were able to weed him out with the podcast. I know he scared you something awful, but he will get his punishment."

"Thank you, Eleanor. I appreciate you." The door chimed. "I better get back to work."

I scurried back behind the counter. Today, it was only me and Fay. Briana was headed out of town for another gig. The two other baristas were college students and with finals approaching soon, they were deep in their studies. While having more hands helped, I was used to handling things alongside Fay.

As I placed the rag back in the kitchen, I caught sight of Fay taking out a rack of croissants from the oven. She'd recently expanded the pastries and sandwiches that she offered. Thursday's special was pimento cheese on croissant.

I washed my hands. "I see you're getting ready for the dinner crowd."

Fay grinned. "We sold out of the specials at lunch. I'm glad I made an extra bowl of the pimento cheese. Everything good up there?"

"Yeah, just one or two folks. I got it."

"Okay, holler if you need me."

One of the benefits of being a small coffee shop and also a staple in the community, customers were willing to wait for service. But we made it worth it. I grinned as I caught sight of the man perusing the pastries behind the glass.

Claude McKnight was a local artist and a regular. We had quite a few of his paintings on display in the café, including one life-size portrait of my grandfather.

"Hey, Claude, you finally came out of your cave."

Crow's feet had begun to emerge around his blue eyes. He wore his blond tresses in his usual man bun. "Yes, after I put down the paint brush it occurred to me that I needed a good cup of coffee. That stuff at my place wasn't doing the trick."

"Well, I will get you fixed up. The usual?"

"Absolutely."

I rang up a large black coffee and a banana nut muffin. By the time I placed the items on the tray, the front door chimed again.

I watched as Claude took his tray to sit by Eleanor, who'd been like a surrogate mother to him.

I drew my attention back to the customer who'd walked in.

My stomach dropped.

Lily approached the counter and the way she glared at me, I had a feeling she had no intentions of placing an order.

Thursday, November 14 at 2:56 p.m.

Despite enjoying my new ride, I had a sense of unease about yesterday's events. In my mind, something didn't feel right about the way Terrell lost his cool when I mentioned Lily's name. The other staff members had rallied around me and Andre to ensure the sale wasn't lost, but I could still vividly remember Terrell's animosity.

My cheeks grew warm as Lily flashed fiery eyes in my direction.

I spoke cautiously, the usual chipper greeting in my voice absent. "Hey, Lily, can I help you?"

"Joss." Lily's voice sounded strained, like she was holding back emotions. "Can I speak with you for a moment?"

I swiveled my head to the side. Fay wheeled the tray of croissants out from the back. She looked up. "Lily, it's so good to see you."

"You too, Fay." Lily smiled tightly, her eyes never leaving mine. "I'm trying to get out like Mom wants me to."

Fay began to load in the tray of fresh croissants. "You give anymore thought to working in the center?"

Lily turned her attention to Fay. "I'm still thinking about it." Lily flickered her eyes toward me and then back toward Fay. "Fay, would you mind if I borrow Joss for a second? You guys don't look super busy."

Fay glanced at me and then Lily. "Um. Okay. It's just the two of us today."

"This won't take long." Lily walked away from the counter.

My boss had questions in her eyes, but I shrugged. I hadn't mentioned what happened at the car dealership yesterday.

I gestured toward the back room. "We can talk back here." The café had an intimate homey vibe to it. While there were tables and booths in the front, toward the back were various sitting areas with large chairs and couches. On occasion, we had college students studying or customers who needed a corner to park with a book during their lunch break. I moved to an area near the window and turned to face Lily.

"I know what this is about."

"Do you?" Lily's eyes flashed with anger. "Because I had an unpleasant visit last night from my... brother-in-law. If I can call him that."

I held up my hands. "Lily, I was buying a car, and I made a terrible mistake when I saw Terrell's last name. I had no idea he was Vince's brother."

Lily's shoulders sagged, and she collapsed into a nearby chair. "So, you're not planning on doing a podcast on Vince?"

My eyes widened in surprise. "What? I'm not working on any podcast right now. Is that what he said?"

Lily placed her hands on top of her head. "He accused me of trying to exploit his brother for some fifteen minutes of fame."

"Look," I said feeling confused and helpless all at the same time. "I test drove a car. I loved it and I wanted to buy it. He helped me fill out the paperwork and I noticed his last name and asked one question. Sure, he mentioned that the folks at Carlson Auto listen to my podcast, but I never mentioned anything about working on a new season. My boyfriend was with me. He'll vouch for me."

She shook her head. "I'm sorry. I shouldn't have assumed. I haven't had to deal with Terrell or any of my husband's family in a few months. It's been quiet. I could actually grieve in peace."

I felt a pang of guilt knowing my careless question had caused this mess. "Lily, I'm so sorry. Can I get you something to drink? My treat. It's the least I can do."

She nodded weakly. "A mint latte would be nice, thank you."

I stepped out to prepare her drink, and Fay intercepted me. Concern etched her face. "Everything okay with Lily?"

"Yeah, just a misunderstanding," I replied.

I set the mint latte in front of Lily. "Is there anything else I can do?"

Lily took a sip of her coffee before answering. "Things have been... tense... since Vince died." She paused, then looked at me curiously. "Are you planning to do another season of your podcast?"

The question caught me off guard. "I... I haven't decided yet. I haven't found the right topic."

Lily nodded thoughtfully. "I've listened to the *Cold Justice* podcast. I like how you always seem to find the truth, to find the culprit."

I shifted uncomfortably. "I'm not really an investigator, Lily. I just try to give people a chance to voice their concerns and remember their loved ones."

"Would you consider doing an episode about Vince?" Lily asked.

I opened my mouth and then shut it as I tried processing her request. "Didn't you just come in here angry with me about the possibility that I could have been planning to do a podcast about your husband?"

Lily peered down into the cup. "Honestly, I was more angry at Terrell for coming by to harass me. You know him and a few others made up their mind that I had something to do with Vince's death. They think I married him to get his life insurance. That wasn't the case at all." She looked at me, her eyes watering. But I didn't think it was sadness. I could feel anger radiating from her again. "I want justice for Vince and I also want my life back. You seem to be good at finding the truth even though you're not really investigating."

I blew out a breath. "Well, if you listened to the podcast, then you're familiar with my format. I really need people willing to let me interview them to have a new season. The way Terrell lost his temper yesterday at a place of business, I'm not sure I want to run across him again."

Lily nodded, a mix of emotions playing across her face. "I understand. Terrell looked up to his big brother. He's hurting. We all are. And we need to know what happened. Someone knows why my husband lost his life last year."

I twisted my fingers. While I felt anxious about moving forward with the podcast, I could also feel excitement building at the possibilities. "Okay, if you're sure, reach out to me on the *Cold Justice Podcast* page on Instagram messenger. We can set something up."

"Can we do the recording at my house?" Lily asked.

My stomach dipped when I glanced up and saw Fay walking toward us. Her glasses were perched on her nose and she had that what-are-you-doing look on her face. "Sure. Look, I probably need to get back to work."

Fay walked up to us with her hands on her hip. "Is everything okay?"

I smiled. "It's fine. I will get back behind the counter while you catch up with Lily." I gave Lily a head nod and ignored my boss's intense stare.

I didn't know what I was getting myself into, but I felt more pumped than I had in a few months. Something about diving into the podcast did that for me.

I prayed that I didn't get in too deep this time around.

Thursday, November 14 at 6:12 p.m.

Fay didn't fuss at me as expected, but as my surrogate big sister, she offered her advice while we worked as a team closing the café. I'd finished wiping down all the tables and restocked the cups and condiments, while Fay prepped her trays of pastries and homemade sandwich bread. Earlier this year, she'd brought an industrial size refrigerator that perfectly housed the dough that would be baked around six o'clock the next morning. I handed her a tray of croissants as she organized them accordingly.

Fay spoke over her shoulder, her voice muffled. "You all need to be careful."

Alarm bells rang inside my head as my body stiffened at Fay's comment. Some of it had to do with where we were inside the kitchen area. I'd been attacked here a few months ago. I'd thrown pans at my assailant in my rush to get away.

"What did you say?" My voice sounded extra high even to my own ears.

Fay's eyes widened as she studied my face. She held up her hands as if she were attempting to calm down a hysterical person. "Look, I think Lily has been needing to tell her side of the story and doing an interview on your podcast is probably good for her. But now that you told me what happened with Terrell at Carlson Auto, I think you and Lily need to use caution."

I'd spilled the tea to Fay about my confrontation with Terrell Hartman. I blew out a breath and focused on dropping my tense shoulders. "Do you think Terrell is dangerous or something?"

"No, that's not what I'm saying." Fay took off her glasses and hooked them on the front of her apron. She had dark circles under her eyes which were often hidden by her large turquoise frames. "You don't know the backstory of how Lily ended up with Vince. There are quite a few people who could be a problem. They already drove Lily to hide away from the world for almost a year. I doubt the poor woman had any real opportunities to grieve in peace."

I crossed my arms, and leaned against the steel island. "Well, give me some information so I don't go in blind. I'm really surprised that Lily did this 180 on me. One minute, I thought she was angry that I might have suggested the podcast about her husband. Once she saw I hadn't suggested it, then it became her big idea."

Fay shook her head. "Honestly, I think Terrell messed up by harassing her. I talked to her before she left. She's tired of being the scapegoat. It wasn't like she was there when Vince's car crashed."

I frowned. "So why is she getting blamed?"

Fay slipped her glasses back on her face. "They argued. Like any couple, Lily blew up at Vince. He didn't want to hear what she had to say and left." Fay tilted her head. "They think someone slammed into him and left him there."

"Well, she didn't get in a car and slam into him. The police would have found that out by now. I'm not understanding the animosity."

Fay looked at me as if she felt sorry for me. "Girlfriend, you really don't know what you're stepping into. Let's just say that the bad feelings originated with Vince's first wife."

"Oh!" My eyebrows shot up at this information. "His first wife?"

"Mm-hmm." Fay walked toward her office and I followed. "You certainly have a lot to catch up on."

I stood in the doorway while Fay pulled out her chair and sat down. "Well, you're not going to leave me hanging, are you?"

"I will tell you what I can, but it's a lot." Fay chuckled. "Let's see, Vince and Marianne Hartman were married about eighteen years. They have one daughter, Allison. The Hartmans are a prominent Charleston family. My home church, Greater Zion, is where all of this drama has taken place. Bishop Emerson Hartman, Vince and Terrell's father, was the pastor at Greater Zion for over a decade, and the brothers grew up as "royalty" at Greater Zion. They could do no wrong. When Vince married Marianne, it was a big deal. Marianne is the daughter of another big time pastor here in Charleston, Bishop James Danvers. I'm sure you know the name, Danvers Funeral Home?"

I nodded. "Yes, I'm familiar."

I wished I'd been taking notes. It dawned on me, after a long day at the café, I would probably not remember any of this.

Fay continued, "Good. Well, let's just say when Vince asked Marianne for a divorce, that was considered front page news. And everybody had something to say about it. Then to make matters worse, almost a year and half later, Vince married Lily.

You can imagine that trio was a hot topic, especially for folks at Greater Zion."

"Wait, so after they were divorced Marianne continued going to Greater Zion?"

Fay rolled her eyes. "Now you see where I'm going with this. I was a few years behind Vince in school, but I remember that he was known as a ladies' man. Vince was a very good looking man, looked like Bishop Hartman. And that man aged like fine wine. Both brothers played in the church band. Vince played the piano and Terrell, the drums. Eventually, Vince became the choir director after the previous one passed away."

Fay stood and stretched her arms. "Vince brought a lot of energy to the church. A lot of young people, especially young women, joined the choir. They didn't seem to care that he was a married man. There were rumors. Always rumors."

My mouth popped open as the implications started to penetrate my tired brain. "Are you saying he cheated on his wife with Lily?"

Fay blew out a breath. "That's not the story that you will hear from Lily. But that's definitely the rumor that swirled around them. Which brings me to another person you need to be aware of—Lily's ex-boyfriend."

Incredulity had me holding my chest as if I were in pain. "Another ex in the mix?"

Fay locked the office door. "Yep. Jake Reaves. But you will have to get the tea on him from Briana. She knows him better than I do since he's one of the founders of Indigo Soul."

I went over to the locker area and grabbed my bag. "Briana told me that Lily used to be in the band. That's where I remember her from. She used to be here for Friday Night Jams."

Fay swung her large bag over her shoulder and I followed her toward the front of the café. "Yes, Indigo Soul was formed by Jake and Lily and some other guy. Jake and Lily were a couple for a number of years, on and off. From what I've heard, it was during one of their off periods that Lily got sucked in by Vince."

"Wow. But she claims she and Vince weren't cheating."

Fay cut the last light out over the dining area and we stepped outside into the brisk fall air. I looked up and down the sidewalk as Fay locked up the café. "Lily believed, or was led to believe, that Vince and Marianne were already divorced when she got involved with him."

We waited for a car to pass before we crossed over to where our cars were parked. "Do you believe her?"

Fay didn't answer until we'd stopped underneath the lamp-posts. My car was next to her Camry. "Lily is more your age. Her mother and I have been friends for a number of years. I met Evelyn back when I was an art teacher and she was the music teacher. I can remember Lily as a teenager. She grew into a pretty woman and according to her mother, she's always loved and craved attention from males. Now that is her mother's opinion, but Lily has made some interesting dating choices. And I do know that she was encouraged to leave Vince alone, despite him pursuing her. But you know some women can be stubborn when it comes to a good looking man with some flare and swag about him."

I frowned. "Sounds like he was a bit older than her. She could have been impressionable. If she's my age, your mind starts getting caught up in the fact that you're approaching your thirties and still not married."

"Very true. And apparently that was some of the back and forth Lily had with her ex Jake. He didn't want to settle down, but she did." Fay pursed her lips. "So, you're starting to see the picture. Someone came along offering her what she wanted."

I shrugged. "I mean that makes sense. Every woman wants their happily ever after."

Fay opened her car door and slung her bag onto the seat. "Yeah, but it's a mistake that Lily is probably deeply regretting." Fay reached up and scratched her head. "I might have a proposition for you, so you can fully get a better idea of the situation."

I eyed her. "What you got?"

The lamppost above was bright and comforting, but sent a glare across Fay's eyes. She turned slightly and I saw something like amusement on her face as she gave me a toothy grin. "What are you doing on Sunday morning?"

I straightened. "Well, my elders would want to see me in church."

Fay grinned. "Maybe it's time you visit Greater Zion. If you want to get a feel for the place where Vince reigned, it's good to meet the players. Sunday happens to be Family and Friends Day."

"That would be cool! Will Lily be there?"

Fay shrugged. "I don't know. She comes occasionally, but sometimes she goes to church with her mom over at Missionary Baptist."

"Oh, yeah. I've been there quite a few times. It's where my friends Leesa and Carmen go. It's also my next door neighbor Ms. Eugeena's home church too."

Fay nodded. "Missionary Baptist is a much smaller church than Greater Zion, just so you're prepared."

"I've passed by it several times, just never been inside." I tilted my head. "And where do you sit in a place that big?"

Fay threw her head back and laughed. "If I'm there on time, I sit mid-way. But if I'm walking in there late, I'm squeezing in the back. No matter the size of a church, there are still prime areas for wandering eyes and whispering tongues."

I laughed. "That's church life. I think sometimes people forget about the love one another part."

"Mmmm, you can say that again. Anyway, Joe will be coming with me and he's an on-time fellow." Fay announced with an eye roll.

A giggle slid out my mouth. Fay didn't like to admit one of her boyfriend's better qualities was keeping her on time. "Alright, I will plan to go to church with y'all on Sunday. I'm not sure if Andre will be caught up on his case, but I'll ask if he can come."

I climbed inside my car feeling immediately comforted by the interior. While it may have been used, Carlson Auto had added a new car fragrance. It did the trick for me. Once I turned the ignition, I waved to Fay, who waited on me in her own car. We had a rule now that we closed together and I left the parking lot first. I'd managed to have a few incidents happen when I was alone after-hours at the café. One resulted in me finding the shop owner next door dead and the other involved me fighting for my life.

I headed toward home. I wasn't sure what I could find out during a church service, but I wondered how well loved the popular choir director had been with the drama surrounding his love life.

Chapter 5
Taking Chances

Saturday, November 16 at 11:00 a.m.

Lily's family home stood out on a quiet street, its Victorian architecture a testament to Charleston's rich history. As I walked up the path, nervousness fluttered in my stomach. After talking to Fay, I had some anxiety about the interview, but I carefully wrote questions in my notebook last night. Right now, the only person other than Lily who knew about the interview was Fay. I hadn't said a word about it to Andre.

Leaving him in the dark wasn't intentional on my part. Unfortunately, being the girlfriend of a homicide detective left me hanging sometimes. Andre caught a case on Thursday evening, which meant we only shared a brief phone call Thursday and Friday night. The first forty-eight hours of an investigation was crucial, and Andre and his partner were hitting a neighborhood early Saturday morning to find potential witnesses.

Here I was getting ready to dive into another case for the *Cold Justice* podcast. He would learn soon enough if we could still meet up tonight for dinner.

I raised my hand to ring the doorbell. It was one of those typical doorbells with a camera on it. Hopefully I looked presentable. I had a bad curly girl hair day this morning, so I'd opted for my usual Afro puff.

I expected Lily to answer the door, but a woman in her early sixties opened the door instead. Her silver hair was pulled back in a neat bun for a Saturday morning. While her sharp eyes assessed me, I made the assumption from the similarities in the woman's face that she was related to Lily.

"You must be Joss Miller." Her tone was crisp. "I'm Evelyn Foster, Lily's mother. Won't you come in?"

"It's nice to meet you, Mrs. Foster."

She stepped aside, allowing me to enter. Mrs. Foster was a tall, formidable woman even with her slim build. I could almost picture her during her teaching days.

Mrs. Foster led me into the living room area where there was a mix of antiques from the couches and chairs to the lamps. Appropriate for this older home was a colorful rug that still had clean marks from a recent vacuum. The older wood floor shined and crackled as we walked further into the room.

Art and music held a favorable place in this home, the walls adorned with family photos and framed sheet music. A large portrait of a younger Lily hung over a fireplace. Dressed in a ballerina tutu and a tiara, young Lily's eyes sparkled as she held her head high.

A singer and a dancer.

"That's a beautiful picture."

Evelyn smiled. "It is. Lily's father painted it from a photograph. It was one of his favorite pieces. His little girl."

A pang softly ripped through my stomach. I assumed Lily was a daddy's girl too. I could relate.

"Lily will be down in a minute," Mrs. Foster said. Concern etched lines around her eyes. "Ms. Miller..."

"Oh, please call me Joss."

"Sure. And you can call me Evelyn. Can I get you anything?"

"No, I'm good. I have bottled water in my bag."

"You've come prepared, Joss. I admired what you did with your podcast for your grandfather. I actually know your grandfather's sisters."

"Oh, you do?"

She chuckled. "Yes, Sugar Creek is a small world. In fact, it was your aunt, Ruth, who taught me the piano. And I had your aunt, Thelma, for English."

"That's awesome. Do you know my next door neighbor? Eugeena Patterson-Jones? She taught Social Studies."

Evelyn's eyes twinkled. "Oh yes, I know Mrs. Patterson. She's one of my other mentors as well. Eugeena and I shared many adventures with our students. You have a lot of good people around you, Joss."

"I do. I feel blessed."

Evelyn turned her head toward the doorway as if she expected Lily. When she turned back to me, the concern was back in her eyes. "I hope you understand the delicacy of this situation. Lily's been through so much... I know she wants her voice heard."

"I understand."

Footsteps moved quickly down the steps outside the living room.

"Joss, you're here. I see you met my mother." Lily glided into the living room, her eyes locked on her mother.

Tension simmered between the two women. Evelyn, in a subtle manner, was trying to make sure this interview wouldn't cause harm to her daughter. I had the feeling the women may have argued, maybe even a few minutes before I arrived.

"Mom, I'm sure Joss needs some quiet for the interview." Lily turned to me. "Are you ready to begin?"

Before I could answer, Evelyn interjected, her voice sharp. "Lily, are you sure about this? You know this is only going to make things worse. Bad enough we had to get a restraining order on that..."

Restraining order? Who? Terrell?

While I was trying to figure out who they were talking about, Lily clasped her hands together in a begging position. "Mom, we've been over this. I need to tell my side of the story."

"Your side?" Evelyn scoffed. "What about Vince's daughter? Or Marianne? Have you thought about how this might affect them?"

"Of course I have!" Lily's voice rose. "I loved Vince too."

Evelyn's eyes flashed. "Did you really? You rushed into marrying him when you barely knew him."

"Here we go again," Lily muttered. "You never approved of any man in my life."

"That's not true," Evelyn retorted. "Jake was a fine young man. At least he wasn't married when you met him."

Lily's face flushed under her caramel skin. "I can't believe you said that. My own mother. Vince was divorced already. And you always gave Jake a hard time because he tried to make a living being a musician. That wasn't good enough for your daughter, even though you're a music teacher." She waved her hands in the air and spun around from her mother muttering, "The irony!"

I shifted uncomfortably in my seat, feeling like an intruder in this family drama. Lily must have noticed my movement. She took a deep breath, visibly trying to calm herself.

"Mom, please," she said, her voice strained. "This is important to me. Can we discuss this later? I don't want to waste Joss's time."

Evelyn's eyes appeared to water and her caramel skin had reddened like her daughter. Without a word, she nodded curtly in my direction and left the living room.

As Evelyn's footsteps echoed on the hardwood floor, I grabbed my water bottle from my bag. I gulped the liquid, watching Lily as she sank down on the couch across from me. She tossed throw pillows to the other side of the couch and then wrapped her arms around one.

I placed the cap back on my bottled water. "We don't have to do this now."

"Yes, we do. Don't you see what I'm up against?" Lily closed her eyes and sighed deeply. When she opened her eyes, I felt all the hurt and pain projected in her gaze. "I'm sorry about that, Joss." Lily sat up still clutching the throw pillow in her arms. "Can we get started?"

I nodded and reached in my bag for my phone and notebook. I couldn't help but wonder if Lily's mother was right. I knew how often my own mother's advice was on point.

COLD JUSTICE PODCAST, EPISODE #11
"A Christmas Eve Tragedy: Part 1"

Joss: Welcome to the *Cold Justice* podcast. I'm your host, Joss Miller. I know, I know. It's been awhile. I'm still learning how to do this podcast thing. If you're a subscriber, thank you so much for sticking with this podcast.

Today, we're diving into a case that shook the Sugar Creek community approximately one year ago—the mysterious death of Vince Hartman, the beloved choir director at Greater Zion.

For those of you not in this area, I want to provide some context about the Hartman family and their deep roots in Charleston's Christian community. Vince Hartman, our victim, came from a prominent local family. His father, Bishop Emerson Hartman, was the pastor at Greater Zion for over a decade before his death.

Vince's role in the church was significant. He started in the church band as a pianist and eventually became the choir director. His charismatic leadership attracted many young people to the choir and to Greater Zion.

I want to remind listeners, this podcast is not about gossip or presenting people in an unfavorable light. I want those seeking justice, especially the victim's family and friends to have a safe platform to share their story about their loved ones.

Initially thought to be a tragic car accident, the police investigation has cast doubt on this conclusion. To help us understand the events of that fateful night, I'm joined by Lily Hartman, Vince's widow. Lily, thank you for being here.

Lily: Thank you for having me, Joss. It's... it's not easy to talk about, but it's been almost a year. I really want to find out what happened to my husband.

Joss: Lily, before we get into the events of that night, I'd like to learn a bit more about your relationship with Vince. Can you tell us how you two first met?

Lily: Of course. Vince and I actually met through his younger sister. I've been friends with her since high school. I thought she was kidding about setting me up with her brother. But she wasn't, and we got along great. Vince and I both loved music. We both played the piano. I guess I finally started to feel like he was the one when we hung out at an event. I was part of a local band called Indigo Soul, and we were performing at the annual Juneteenth event. Vince was there with the Greater Zion choir. I was so moved by his performance and how he electrified the choir and audience. He was so passionate about music – not just gospel music either. It was impossible not to be drawn to him.

Joss: I understand you two were still newlyweds. How long were you together before you got married?

Lily: (quiet for a few seconds) Vince and I had a whirlwind romance. We dated for about a year before Vince proposed. He, um, was coming out of a divorce and I wanted to make sure I wasn't a rebound (laughs). We had a short three month engagement, and then a small, intimate wedding on New Year's Eve.

Joss: Vince Hartman was kind of like royalty in some circles. How did you find adjusting to such a prominent family in the church community?

Lily: It was... challenging at first. I grew up in church, one much smaller than Greater Zion. My mom still attends Missionary Baptist to this day. Greater Zion was welcoming, but... Look, I'm no heathen, but I'm not an everyday Sunday gal. I've been singing in a band for several years instead of the church choir. There's a difference. Vince was incredibly supportive though, always encouraging me to be myself.

Joss: Can you tell us a bit about Vince as a person? What was he like outside of his role as choir director?

Lily: Vince was... he was larger than life. He had this infectious enthusiasm for everything he did. At home, he was always humming or playing the piano. He loved to cook and would often invite the whole choir over for big dinners. He loved people and people loved him.

Joss: It sounds like he was a wonderful person. Now, I know this might be difficult. But can you tell us about your life together in the months leading up to last Christmas Eve?

Lily: (takes a deep breath) They were difficult to be honest. Vince and I were struggling to find our balance. His family, his ex-wife and his daughter, they were a constant source of tension between us. There were always snide comments, little digs about my past with the band and how people really thought Vince and I met.

Joss: That is awful. How did Vince handle these family dynamics? He had to know this was difficult for you.

Lily: Vince... he tried to keep the peace. He was caught in the middle, you know? He wanted to make everyone happy — me, his family. But in trying to please everyone, I think he ended up pleasing no one. We argued about it a lot. I felt like he wasn't standing up for me, and he felt like I wasn't trying hard enough with his family.

Joss: Is that what the argument was about last Christmas Eve?

Lily: Yes. (voice trembling) Vince wanted us to go to his parents' house for dinner. The whole family would be there. I just... I couldn't face it. Another evening of cold stares and backhanded comments. We had a huge argument about it. I told him to go without me, that I was tired of trying to fit into a family that clearly didn't want me there. He left angry, saying I was being selfish and ruining Christmas. (pauses) That was the last time I saw him alive.

Joss: I'm so sorry, Lily.

Lily: I've been learning to cope and appreciate the short time that we had together.

Joss: You know, reports say Vince didn't go in the direction of his family home. The car accident was several miles away. Was there another place or someone else he might have visited?

Lily: I've thought about it a lot. He had been agitated or annoyed for weeks. I thought maybe the pressure of family, church and the holiday season was getting to him. Earlier that day, I overheard him having a heated phone conversation, but he brushed it off when I asked about it. To be honest, Vince was the kind of man who attracted female attention. He certainly got mine (laughs nervously). My insecurities and listening to others led me to believe some horrible things.

Joss: Did you think he was involved with someone?

Lily: That's what others wanted me to believe. But we were happy. Other than outside relationships, we were good.

Joss: I know this must be hard. What else can you share?

Lily: It's still surreal, even almost a year later. When I woke up, I noticed Vince never came home. I'd left a lot of messages on his phone and had just made coffee when the doorbell rang. There were detectives at my door, and I knew it was bad. They asked to come in, and said Vince's car had gone off the road on Route 17. By the time they found him... he was gone.

Joss: The initial report suggested it was an accident, but something changed after further investigation.

Lily: Yes. This was no accident. The police found skid marks suggesting Vince had swerved suddenly, but there was no apparent reason for him to do so. Later, they found paint on the back of his car and a broken taillight, like someone slammed into him, causing him to lose control of the car. Whoever did it didn't stop to help him or call for help. Who would do that?

Joss: It's awful that someone could be that heartless.

Lily: Police said it could have been a drunk driver and they may not remember. They would have had damage to their car.

Joss: And how did Vince's family react to all this?

Lily: (sighs) They... they blamed me. They found out Vince and I argued and thought he might have been upset or distracted while driving. But I know there was more to it. Vince was hiding something, and I think it had to do with his death. Why would he not go straight to his family's house? They were expecting us...well, him to arrive.

Joss: Did Vince mention anything to you about feeling threatened or worried about something?

Lily: Not directly, but looking back, there were signs. There was that phone call I overheard. I feel like there may have been other instances of him getting off the phone too quickly, but that day stands out. I play that entire day and evening over and over in my mind. (voice breaking) I keep thinking, if I had just gone with him, maybe things would have been different. Maybe he wouldn't have... (trails off)

Joss: (pauses) Thank you, Lily. I admire your courage and willingness to share with our audience.

Lily: Thank you for letting me be on the podcast. I've been wanting to talk about his death. Vince was a force and I don't want him forgotten.

Joss: Hey, listeners, if you have any information about Vince Hartman's case, even the smallest detail, be sure to contact the CPD with your tips.

If you're interested in sharing your experience with Vince, send me a DM on the Instagram podcast page. I would love to talk to you.

This is Joss Miller, and you're listening to the *Cold Justice* podcast.

Saturday, November 16 at 6:34 p.m.

The aroma of garlic and herbs filled Andre's kitchen as I set the table. Music played softly from the Bose speakers on Andre's entertainment system. I recognized the oldie and swayed to the melody as Usher crooned "U Got It Bad." I was enjoying the song so much, I didn't realize Andre had come up behind me. I gasped in delight when he wrapped his arms around me.

"Hey, babe," Andre said, leaning in for a quick kiss. "Man, I have missed being with you. Sorry I've been MIA the past few days."

I turned so I could look up into his eyes. A familiar warmth spread through my chest. "No worries. I'm just glad we're getting some time together now."

He kissed me again. "We should eat before we get into other things."

We settled at the dining table and piled our plates high with pasta. Andre asked, "So, what have you been up to while I've been chasing leads?"

I hesitated, but then reached for my phone. "It might be best if you listen." I tapped the screen. "I went to visit Lily Hartman today."

Andre's brow furrowed in confusion as my voice filled the room.

"Welcome to the Cold Justice podcast. I'm your host, Joss Miller. Today, we're diving into a case that shook the Sugar Creek community exactly one year ago—the mysterious death of Vince Hartman..."

Andre's fork clattered against his plate. "Pause it," his voice was tight.

His anger surprised me. So I hit the pause button. "What's wrong?"

He stared at me, disbelief etched across his face. "Joss, do you understand what you're doing?"

I opened my mouth to explain, but Andre cut me off. "I admired you for doing the podcast about your grandfather. I even thought it was cool when you wanted to pay tribute to Rebecca Montgomery. But..." He closed his eyes and took a breath. "That guy came after you."

It felt like Andre's eyes blazed into mine. Suddenly feeling heated, I placed my own fork on the table. "I know—"

"You're going to stir people up, maybe the wrong person." Andre interrupted. "You say you're not investigating, but that's exactly what you're doing. This murder, even if it was a year ago, is still fresh. Emotions are running high. Remember how Terrell reacted at the car dealership?"

"Of course." Appetite gone, I twisted my fingers, recalling the tense encounter earlier this week.

Andre continued, his voice softening, "That still bothers me how he just went off like that. I hated having to go all protective, but I've seen grown men lose control."

Unfortunately, so have I.

I didn't want this. The last thing I wanted was to fight with Andre, so I tried to lighten the mood. "You wouldn't have really fought him. You're a cop."

Andre's eyes met mine, his gaze still intense. "You must not understand how I feel about you, Joss. I would do whatever I have to do to protect you."

I gulped, my cheeks were probably glowing red. "Don't you think Lily deserves someone in her corner? She wants to know what happened to her husband. Look, Terrell harassed her and it was my fault. I needed to make up for that."

I stared at my barely touched plate of pasta, my appetite completely gone. Andre had only managed a few bites himself.

"I'm going to wash the dishes. You can listen to the rest of the podcast. Listen to Lily. Nobody else is listening to her and she was the victim's wife. That's not fair, especially since they were barely married a year."

I quickly gathered up our mostly full plates and retreated to the kitchen, feeling Andre's eyes on me. This was one time I wished he didn't have an open concept home.

I could have stacked the dishes in the dishwasher, but chose to fill the sink with hot, soapy dish water. The waste of good food bothered me, but there was no salvaging this dinner. It felt safer to be in my thoughts with my back turned. I needed a moment. I understood Andre's desire to protect me, but I was my own woman.

I scrubbed the dishes with more force than necessary with Andre's words echoing in my mind. I didn't want to admit it, but he may have been right. I did want to know the truth. Maybe it was time to stop pretending I was so different from other true crime podcasters. After all, I was the girl who always loved a good mystery, whether a book or a crime show. I liked trying to figure out whodunits.

As I dried my hands, I heard the outro playing from the other room.

So, he listened to it.

TYORA MOODY

I took a deep breath, steeling myself for the conversation to come. Andre had moved to the couch and had his feet up on the coffee table. I plopped down on the other side of the couch and placed the throw pillow between us.

Tentative, I asked, "Well, what did you think?"

Andre sighed and ran a hand across his low cut hair. I detected he still was concerned by the way his eyes roamed over my face.

"It's... well done, Joss. I can't deny that. You've got a way of getting people comfortable enough to talk to you. Mrs. Hartman has valid reasons for wanting the truth." He paused. "Still, I'm a cop and I'm worried. You're diving into a case that's not been solved, but it's not quite as cold as you think. The podcast could stir up a lot of trouble. With what you just went through and with the grand jury hearing coming up Monday, are you sure you really should be doing this?"

I sighed. "You know the weird thing is for a while it was nice to not think about something else. And I know this is a weird way to move on, but I never intended the podcast to be this one-time thing about my grandfather's murder. So you're right, I need to stop saying I'm not investigating. The folks listening to the podcast want to know the truth. And I do too."

86

Andre leaned forward, his elbows on his knees. "And that's what scares me. You're becoming an amateur investigator. We've already seen how dangerous that can be."

"But I learned a lesson."

He narrowed his eyes as he cocked his head to the side. "Yea? What's that?

"That you can't trust anyone, which I hate to say. But I do want to talk to more people, Andre. I want to know why people were so set on blaming Lily."

He reached over and yanked the throw pillow from in between us. "So, you're not taking her word either. That's good. There's been no proof of her involvement, but please, promise me you'll be careful. And if you find out anything—anything at all that seems off—you come to me first. Okay?"

His eyes searched mine, so intense I felt my heartbeat in my chest. I moved closer to him and he slid an arm around me.

"Don't worry. I will."

I wasn't taking any chances this time.

Chapter 6
Mega-Trouble

Sunday, November 17 at 10:40 a.m.

I'd seen the megachurch structure from afar, but I'd never been this close. Greater Zion's modern architecture was a far cry from the smaller churches I usually attended with family or friends. But what surprised me more was the number of cars already in parking spaces and the long line snaking in to grab a spot. If anyone driving by wasn't aware the building was a church, they may have thought this was a coliseum with people attending a sporting event or a concert.

Andre was planning to come with me, but another homicide case struck last night. I felt extremely blessed to have Andre in my life, but the toll his profession took on our relationship was definitely a downside. Another downside was the tension my podcast seemed to cause, and while I understood his concerns about the topic I was pursuing, he'd known from the beginning

I had an interest in true crime. Despite what I'd gone through this past summer, I wasn't going to let that change me.

At least I was going to try.

Unfamiliar with my surroundings, I followed the car ahead of me. A team of men with brightly colored vests, expertly pointed directing the traffic. With the guidance of one of the parking lot attendants, I eased my car into a space. I hadn't even turned the engine off yet and wondered how I would get out of this massive parking lot.

I blew out a breath. "Okay, Lord. I'm here to praise and worship you." No matter what went down today, Sunday was dedicated to the Lord.

The morning air was a bit nippy, actually feeling like a real autumn day in Charleston. My aqua blue knit dress felt warm and cozy. And, since the weather was cooperating, I let my curls hang across my shoulders. I checked the mirror to make sure I hadn't managed to rub lipstick across my teeth. Somehow, I still looked presentable despite my early morning trek in traffic and arriving to a packed parking lot. I stepped out of my car feeling grateful I'd opted for cute but reasonable heels for walking. The entrance seemed awfully far away.

An older man drove by on a golf cart carrying two older women decked out in their finest. With a quick glance, I caught sight of their heels. They were definitely not suitable for hiking through the parking lot to the church entrance. I followed the stream of parishioners, hoping to run into Fay. After passing several rows of cars, I finally spotted a white Camry and hoped it was Fay's. I felt a wave of relief when a bald-headed man popped up near the car.

It was Fay's boyfriend, Joe Phillips, which meant Fay had to be nearby. A few seconds later, I glimpsed Fay. They'd parked way ahead of me and must have been sitting in the car. I quickly moved in their direction, not wanting to walk into Greater Zion alone.

Joe saw me coming and waved his hand.

Fay turned and smiled as I approached. She held her arms out toward me. "Look at you. You look so pretty this morning and got your hair down too. I only see you in the Sugar Creek Café uniform, so I almost didn't recognize you."

I hugged her. "I can say the same about you, Boss. I love the dress."

Fay wore a red coatdress that was belted at the waist. Since we were always around coffee and food, she also wore her hair pulled up. This morning her locs fell past her shoulders, the tips almost touching her waist. I hadn't realized they were so long.

"This is your first time at Greater Zion. What do you think so far?" Fay asked, linking her arm with mine.

I could feel my eyes stretch as we got in a line moving briskly into the church. "It's... bigger than I expected."

Joe chuckled. "Wait till you see inside."

Fay nodded. "Believe it or not, there's even more people today since it's Family and Friends Day. Let's head in and find some seats."

Like any church, ushers greeted us at the door handing out programs with white gloved hands. Greater Zion had a large lobby with beige, patterned carpeting. Several doors were open down a long hallway, each leading into the sanctuary. I could see rows of people in seats as we moved forward.

I blinked when we stepped inside. It was so much to take in. The sanctuary was a sea of people, and the buzz of conversation filled the air. Greater Zion's seating arrangement was like the inside of a coliseum, the burgundy covered seats sloped down to a large stage. We found seats close to the back, and I was kind of grateful. I had a thing about heights and didn't want to keep stepping down the aisle through the crowds.

The band started with an up-tempo song. Two large screens on either side of the pulpit area zoomed in on the band members. There were two guitar players, a piano player and a drummer. As the upbeat gospel tune filled the space, I couldn't help but imagine how it would have been with Vince Hartman on stage leading the choir. The worship team closed with a modernized version of "How Great Thou Art."

I looked around as some type of transition began. The screens showed a really large choir waiting in the wings on either side of the pulpit. Dressed in black, instead of the more traditional choir robes, their voices rang out as they marched in from both sides filling the rows behind the pulpit. A woman came and stood in front of the choir. Her presence was commanding even though she hadn't opened her mouth yet.

Everyone around us, including Fay and Joe stood. Not familiar with the order of service, I stood too. A hush rippled over the mass of people. It was amazing how still and quiet the sanctuary had become in a matter of seconds.

The woman who stood center stage opened her mouth. I had to make sure I closed my own mouth which dropped open. Her voice was stunning, a soprano. The hairs on my arm stood. I soon forgot about the large number of people around me and just enjoyed her voice as the choir sang the chorus.

The pastor led a lineup of other ministers onto the pulpit. He greeted the congregation and led us in prayer. After the prayer, we all sat down.

I leaned toward Fay. "Who was the lead singer?"

Fay's eyebrows rose. "That was Marianne Hartman, Vince's first wife."

"Marianne Hartman..." I echoed. "Wow. She has a beautiful voice."

"She's one of the best," Fay said with a knowing smile. "You're going to learn a lot today, but also some of God's word too."

"That's what I'm here for." I needed my cup filled for the week. The grand jury hearing loomed tomorrow. I needed to cast all my anxieties on the Lord.

As the announcements began, I looked around the packed sanctuary again. This time I felt a prickling sensation. The kind you get when someone's eyes are on you. I turned my head and caught sight of Terrell Hartman a few rows down. His scowl was unmistakable, but his eyes weren't on me.

Lily Hartman smiled at an usher as she took a program.

Hmmm, this is about to be interesting.

Surely folks knew how to behave on the Lord's day.

Sunday, November 17 at 11:16 a.m.

Lily glanced around, looking a bit lost until Fay waved to her. A relieved smile spread across Lily's face as she made her way toward us. Joe, Fay and I scooted over another seat to make room. As Lily settled in beside me, I noticed Terrell's gaze had shifted, now alternating between Lily and me. I couldn't help but think that the man needed to get it together – this was church, after all.

The man sitting next to Terrell glanced back at us. His face looked familiar to me. That's when I realized it was Terrell's co-worker, KJ. He said something to Terrell, who turned his attention back to the service. I was thankful to not have those intense eyes on us.

The woman doing the announcements asked newcomers to stand.

Panic made my empty stomach do cartwheels. I looked over at Fay.

She grinned at me. "All you have to do is stand. There's too many people to introduce yourself individually."

With a sigh of relief, I stood along with a host of other newcomers. We were welcomed and encouraged to stay after services for the Family and Friends Day meal. That sounded good to me. I wished again that Andre could have come with me.

As the choir struck up another song, my ears perked up. I turned to Lily. "Your voice is so beautiful. You should be down there singing."

She smiled at me. "Thank you for saying that. I used to be in the choir when Vince was alive, but I'm fine right here for now."

My brows furrowed. Vince's ex-wife and current wife in the choir together. I wanted to dive into that scenario a bit more but reminded myself I was supposed to be enjoying praise and worship. My questions would have to wait until a more appropriate time.

I found myself drawn into the pastor's sermon and had already decided I would return again. It was easy to see why Vince had been so passionate about his role here. As I looked around, I noticed there were a lot more younger people, many my age. When I went to church with my mother and great aunts, I often felt like the youngest adult present. The closest age range after me was a group of bored teenagers that sat in the back.

After the benediction, the aisles filled with chatty congregants. But many made a beeline toward the exits. I followed Lily out of the aisle. With Fay and Joe behind us, we exited through the door we came in. But instead of heading outside, we moved with the crowd. It didn't take long for me to understand why.

The scent of fried chicken summoned us all. As we drew closer, I detected another meat too – ham.

Joe and I must have been thinking the same. He rubbed his hands together. "Oh, this is going to be like having Thanksgiving early."

Fay smacked his arm. "Okay. Calm down. You're acting like you haven't eaten in days."

"Well, it has been about almost twelve hours. That's half a day." Joe mused.

Lily and I giggled at the two of them bickering in front of us.

"Lily Hartman." A soft Southern drawl drifted from behind us. I turned to find a sharply dressed woman in a soft pink suit. The outfit fit her perfectly, conservative yet feminine. Her warm smile and almond eyes made her appear demure. She glanced at me before reaching out to Lily, curiosity in her eyes.

Lily smiled politely and bent down for an awkward hug with the tiny woman. "Sophia. It's been awhile."

"Lily, it's so good to see you out," the woman gushed. "We've missed you and your voice in the choir. Are you thinking of coming back?"

Lily's smile faltered. "I... I don't think so, Sophia."

As they chatted, I caught sight of Marianne Hartman sitting down at a table flanked by a teenage girl. I assumed this was her daughter with Vince. But I didn't have time to study them, the line was moving pretty fast. I noticed most people in line elected to grab take-out boxes. When Fay and Joe didn't grab a take-out container, I assumed they wanted to stay and fellowship. Since I was visiting with Fay, I definitely didn't want to make the hike back to my car alone.

My nose was on the money. There was fried chicken, a known staple at most church functions, and sliced ham as well. Since I opted to skip breakfast, I had both meats along with string beans, macaroni and cheese and a roll. I juggled my full plate and a cup of iced tea. The dessert table offered various slices of cake, but I wasn't taking any chances. Joe had found a table for all of us.

Lily sat on the other side of me, still chatting with the woman named Sophia. I settled in. There was an art to eating fried chicken in front of people, at least for me. I daintily tried to tear pieces of chicken off with my fork while attempting to eavesdrop.

"Is there anything I can do, Lily?" Sophia asked, concern etched on her face.

Lily hesitated, then gestured toward me. "Actually, Joss here is the host of the *Cold Justice* podcast. We're trying to find out what really happened to Vince."

With my mouth full, I did my best to swallow and not give Lily a look.

Did she really need to announce that in here?

Sophia's eyes widened as she turned her attention to me. "Oh! I love your podcast!" Tears welled up. "I've known Vince since we were kids. He was... he was such a wonderful man."

I covered my mouth and chewed as quickly as I could. I wanted to respond without being gross. "Yeah, I'd love to hear more about your experiences with Vince. Would you be willing to do an interview for the podcast?"

Sophia's eyes darted to Lily and then back to me. Her bright smile began to dim. "Oh, I... I'm not sure. I wouldn't want to upset Marianne."

Lily's posture stiffened, her voice tight. "Marianne should want to know what happened to her daughter's father too."

I didn't want to cause any friction between the two women. "I understand your hesitation. If you change your mind and want to do the interview, feel free to DM me on the podcast's Instagram page. No pressure at all."

Sophia nodded, "Sure, maybe we could talk." She reached out to touch Lily's arm. "You know I will help if I can."

Lily reached for her ice tea. "I know you will. We all loved—" Before Lily could finish her words, someone bumped her from behind. Liquid from the cup in her hand sloshed onto the table.

Her complexion reddened and she turned, her mouth opened to say something. But the words seemed to die on her lips.

I turned to glimpse the person who'd caused the accident.

It was a young girl. The teen I'd seen earlier sitting at the table with Marianne. Her slanted eyes and chocolate skin favored her father's face.

From the smirk on her face, the girl meant to start trouble.

Sunday, November 17 at 1:34 p.m.

Both Fay and I reached for our extra napkins and helped Lily mop up the stream of tea before it reached the floor. The tension in the air was palpable as Vince's daughter remained standing as if to monitor the mess she'd helped cause. What parent would allow a child to show this level of rudeness, especially in a church setting of all places?

Probably noticing the commotion, Marianne appeared beside her daughter, her face a mixture of concern and irritation. "Allison," Marianne said, her voice low but stern. "What's going on here?"

Allison flinched and her smirk faded. "Nothing, Mom. Just an accident." The girl looked over at Lily, her eyes now nervous.

Lily dabbed at her wet sleeve with a napkin. For a moment, it seemed like she might say something. There seemed to be a silent exchange between Lily and the teenager. Whatever was on Lily's mind stayed a secret as her expression softened. She glanced at Marianne. "It's fine. No harm done."

Fay, however, wasn't having it. My boss was not one to hold her tongue. She turned to Allison and held up a sopping napkin. "Young lady, I think you owe Lily an apology. Accidents happen, but we should always take responsibility for our actions. Would you mind getting us some more napkins?"

Allison looked down, shuffling her feet. "Sorry," she mumbled, barely audible. "I didn't mean to bump into your chair. I'll get some more napkins." The girl trotted off quickly.

While looking at her retreating back, I noticed the volume seemed to have dropped considerably in the fellowship hall. Some people were looking furtively in our direction without trying to be obvious, while others were gawking and waiting for more of the show.

Lily shared my red-boned complexion. Right now, her cheeks and nose were slightly red. If I were in her shoes, this would have been embarrassing for me too.

Lily smiled, but her eyes were wary. "Like I said, it's fine." She looked toward Marianne. "It's good to see you, Marianne."

Really? I wouldn't think it would be good seeing the first wife.

The thought entered my mind before I could stop it.

Marianne didn't smile back, as though she had a similar thought. Her shoulders seemed set like she was ready to defend her daughter. This didn't appear to be the same woman I saw singing like an angel about an hour ago.

Allison returned with a pile of napkins. She stood looking unsure about what to do next.

Since she stood closest to me, I held out my hands. "Thank you."

Marianne's eyes fell on me as her daughter handed me the napkins. As if she'd snapped out of a trance, Marianne glanced around and then placed her hands on her daughter's shoulders. The girl grimaced at her mom's touch.

"I hope you're doing well, Lily." She turned her body slightly away from Lily to address Fay. There was a much more friendlier tone to her voice now. "Fay, it's that time of year again. You doing that pumpkin spice thing at the café?"

Fay nodded. "Of course. It's what people want. We're doing it for a limited time up until Thanksgiving. Be sure to stop in." She tilted her head to the side. "I haven't seen you in a while."

Marianne blew out a breath. "Well, I hate to sound macabre at this celebration, but as you know, my family is in the business of taking care of people's homegoing services. And that business is always booming."

I recalled Fay telling me Marianne's family owned Danvers Funeral Home. With the mounting homicide cases my detective boyfriend investigated, I wasn't surprised business was booming.

Sophia, who had been watching the exchange with concern, spoke up. "Marianne, have you met Joss?"

Marianne looked at me, her eyes curious now. "No. Joss... What's your last name? We might be a big church but we still like to know everyone's kin. You look like someone I know."

I laughed uneasily. "Joss Miller."

Marianne cocked her head. "I know some Millers. Who's your parents?"

This was definitely a Southern thing. People had to know your kinfolk. I guess people were looking to see if they were related or something. "My mother is Clarice Miller. My dad was David Miller. He passed away ... almost ten years ago now."

Marianne slid into funeral director mode and touched my hand, "I'm sorry, honey. Your mama is an accountant."

I shouldn't have been surprised she knew my mother. Clarice Miller was a quiet woman who kept to herself, even more so after my dad died. But she was a pretty popular person, especially at the first of the year and up until the end of tax season.

I nodded, "She does a lot of taxes for people."

Marianne threw her head back and laughed. "She helps me out throughout the year with the funeral home books. I knew you looked like someone I knew; I can see her features in your face. Where do you work?"

I wasn't sure why, but Marianne seemed to want to keep the conversation going with me. I glanced over at Lily, I had no doubt she was probably listening. "I work at Sugar Creek Café."

Fay responded, "She's my assistant manager."

Marianne clasped her hands together. "Oh my. That's nice to have some good help."

Sophia, who'd been quiet, spoke, "She's also a podcaster too. Isn't that wonderful?"

Allison, who, up until that point, looked bored and ready to bolt, looked at me with interest. "You have a podcast?"

Before I could respond, Sophia answered, "A true crime podcast. The *Cold Justice* podcast In fact, she's investigating Vince's death."

Marianne's eyes widened, then narrowed as she looked at me. "Investigating? The police already failed and probably have forgotten at this point. What can a podcast do?"

Lily, still blotting her wet sleeve, stated. "Sometimes fresh eyes can uncover new information. Don't you want to find out the truth?"

Marianne spun back toward Lily, her face hardened. "The truth? The truth is that my hu... ex-husband died in a tragic accident. I'm afraid you're reopening old wounds."

Allison frowned. "But Mom, Dad's death wasn't an accident."

Marianne grabbed Allison's arm. "That's enough. We're leaving." She turned back to us. "Please, let this go. Vince did enough while he was alive. Let him rest in peace. We certainly need peace too."

As Marianne led Allison away, I could see the hurt and confusion on the girl's face. Why wouldn't Marianne want to help her daughter find some peace with her father's death? I still missed my dad something awful, but I knew what took him away from me.

Cancer.

Lily appeared drained. She pushed her plate of uneaten food away.

"I'm sorry," Sophia said. "I didn't mean to cause a scene. I can talk too much sometimes."

Lily shook her head. "It's fine. You were right, Marianne was going to be upset about it."

I frowned, wondering why Sophia brought it up if she knew it would upset Marianne. That seemed a strange thing to do.

Before I could give it anymore thought, I caught sight of a familiar face approaching our table. Since it was Sunday, it took me a moment to place him. But I wondered if the man ever dressed bad.

Grant Carlson, the man from the car dealership, slipped into a seat next to Sophia. "Everything fine over here, folks? Y'all are quite the popular table."

Sophia giggled. "Oh, honey, you're just making things up. We were just having a conversation. Have you met Joss?"

Why was this woman determined to introduce me to everyone like I was some celebrity?

She turned to me, "Joss, this is my husband Grant Carlson."

Seeing Grant and Sophia together, I couldn't help but admire what a striking couple they made.

"I've already met Ms. Miller," Grant greeted me with a warm smile. "How are you enjoying your car?"

"I love it. Thanks again for all your help last week."

"I'm glad to hear that," Grant said. "If you need anything at all, don't hesitate to reach out."

Sophie giggled again. "Oh my goodness. I should have known. Everybody knows you, Grant. Half of Sugar Creek gets their cars from Carlson Auto."

Grant chuckled. "It's what keeps you living like a queen, Mrs. Carlson."

I glanced over at Fay, who gave a subtle eye roll and began stacking their plates. Joe stood and grabbed all our plates.

Grateful for the meal, I said goodbye to Lily and the Carlsons, promising to return to Greater Zion another time.

When we stepped out into the parking lot, the sun was high in the sky indicating we'd been in the building for most of the afternoon. I let out an audible sigh of relief.

Fay fell into step beside me as Joe hurried toward the car.

She hooked her arm in mine, "Well, now you've met Greater Zion's royal families – the Hartmans and the Carlsons."

"They were all very interesting."

Fay stopped at the row where her car was parked. "You sure you want to pursue this for your podcast?"

I shrugged. "I've already interviewed Lily, and it's out there now that I'm doing it. I don't know who else will want to talk to me, so we'll see."

Fay glanced back at the church building. "I don't think you're going to have a hard time finding people who want to talk about Vince Hartman."

I had a feeling she was right about that. But I was curious about the people who didn't want to talk about him. One of those people being his ex-wife.

In the few minutes I'd spent with her, I could tell Marianne kept a lot underneath the surface. What else was she hiding behind that polished funeral director facade? There seemed to be so many unspoken feelings about her ex-husband and his second wife — feelings that ran deeper than she was willing to show.

Chapter 7

Crime Never Sleeps

Sunday, November 17 at 7:38 p.m.

I sat on the couch balancing my MacBook precariously on my knees while uploading the episode with Lily. I wasn't sure yet if I wanted to call this a new season. For one, I wasn't sure who else would talk to me. Over the past few months, I'd listened to other true crime podcasts, some with well over a hundred podcasts. Many numbered their episodes and kept it going. One popular podcaster featured a different cold case each week, while another dived deep into one case for several weeks.

Based on my research, I edited my earlier episodes, renaming and renumbering them. I couldn't imagine doing these weekly, but I knew that's how you kept an engaged audience.

Episode #11, here we are.

I was definitely still an amateur at this podcast thing, but I'd managed to help crack two murder cases, one cold case and one that happened next door to the café. And I'd almost managed to lose my own life.

Although that was not really something to brag about.

But people seemed to open up to me. Lily certainly didn't mind spilling her guts to my questions. Today, after the run-in with her stepdaughter and her husband's first wife at Greater Zion, I hoped neither Lily nor I would regret my scheduled release in the morning.

I removed the headphones from my ear and tossed them next to me on the couch. I glanced over at my grandmother Louise in her favorite armchair. Her eyes were glued to the most modern furniture in the room, a fifty-five inch flat screen television. In her lap sat the oldest cat in the house, appropriately named Ginger. Ginger was too old to live up to the notoriety that came with being an orange cat. This evening, the tuxedo cats, Mickey and Minnie were dozing next to each other. All of them had been fed and were lounging around in the living room with their human housemates.

I still hadn't been able to talk Louise into letting go of cable television. She claimed it was much easier to flip to the channels she's always enjoyed than try out a streaming service. It was fine. I kept my subscriptions to Netflix, Hulu, and various others on and off when I wanted to watch the latest trending show. For now, I was content with watching whatever Louise watched.

Louise glanced over at me, a twinkle in her eyes. Despite being in her seventies, Louise always looked ready to get into something. She'd been the neighborhood watch chairperson for many years and for good reason. Louise Hopkins stayed on top of what was going on around her. And she enjoyed me staying with her.

My mother, Louise's biological daughter, kept asking me when I was going to move out. I think my mother expected me to move in with Andre, like I had with past boyfriends. But Andre hadn't even suggested it, even though I've spent the night at his place several times. I explained to my mother, and anyone who would listen, that Andre was different. He grew up around women and he was the most gentleman of men. He was also a faith driven man. I often wondered how he was able to hold to his convictions and still work homicide cases. I sensed the work took a toll on him.

Louise's voice broke into my thoughts. "Are you ready for tomorrow?"

For a brief moment, I thought my grandmother was referring to the podcast I was scheduling for release at six o'clock in the morning. But then I remembered the other important appointment at ten o'clock.

Oh, yeah. The grand jury.

My stomach lurched at the thought. I'd been so entangled with Vince Hartman and the people around him the past few days that I'd forgotten. Well, not so much forgot but pushed it out of my mind.

"I guess so. Andre told me it's just the prosecutor and the jury. No judge or anything."

Louise nodded. "Is Andre available to drive you? You shouldn't go over there by yourself."

I sat up. "I hadn't thought about it."

Louise reached for her phone which she kept by her. My grandmother might be up in age, but she enjoyed being on her iPhone like a young person. Mainly, she liked to be on Facebook, but she was able to respond and send a text, which could be a real hoot. I usually had to decipher what she was trying to say with all the missing words or where the phone had decided to spell a word for her.

I frowned as Louise tapped on someone in her contacts. "Who are you calling?"

"Eugeena. Maybe her or Amos can go with you."

Before I could protest, Louise had already started talking. This was supposed to be kind of a hush ordeal. Not everyone in the world needed to know I was testifying before a grand jury tomorrow. I sighed and sank onto the couch. The only girl cat in the house, Minnie glided across the top of the couch and climbed into my lap.

"Thank you, girl." I rubbed her soft fur appreciating that the cat picked up on my emotions.

Louise chattered loudly probably due to the fact that the volume on the television was loud. It hadn't bothered me since I'd been wearing my noise-canceling headphones the last hour.

"Oh, that would be wonderful. I will let Joss know. We appreciate it." Louise looked down at the phone and remembered to press the end call button. She grinned at me, her rosy cheeks made her look like a chipmunk. "Eugeena said you should call Leesa. She's off tomorrow and can probably go with you for support."

"On her day off? She needs her time to herself." My friend Leesa was still a newlywed and had two young children. If she took time off from work, it could have been for one of the kids.

I didn't have long to mull it over before the network went into motion. Leesa sent me a text.

I sighed as I read it.

Leesa: Why didn't you tell me you needed me to take you to the courtroom tomorrow?

Joss: I was going to drive myself. My grandmother decided I needed a driver.

Leesa: Well, I'm glad your grandmother has some sense. What time should I pick you up?

Joss: I have to be there at 10:00 a.m.

Leesa: Traffic is going to be a beast. Let's plan to leave at 9:00 a.m.

Joss: Are you sure? It's your day off.

Leesa: Girl, it will be fine. It's just some comp time from when I went to the conference last month. I had no plans at all!

I found that hard to believe, but I appreciated my friend.

Joss: TY, girl. I will see you in the morning.

I put my phone down and went back to rubbing the cat who'd been eyeing my exchange on the phone. A pleased purr rumbled from her as I looked at the television which showed one of Charleston's anchorwomen.

"In local news, a hit-and-run incident has left one man dead in downtown Charleston. We go out to the scene where Maxine Stone is reporting."

Hit-and-run.

My fingers froze over the feline's fur. Minnie nudged my hand with her nose. Trying to multitask, I obediently went back to rubbing the cat, but tuned in to listen to the newscast.

The reporter stood outside, police lights flashed behind her. "Around six o'clock this evening, a passerby found an African American male laying by the side of the road. His injuries suggest that he may have been hit by a car. We're waiting on the victim to be identified, which will happen when police can reach out to next-of-kin. Police are asking for any witnesses to come forward."

"Oh my," Louise exclaimed, shaking her head. "Such a shame. That poor family lost a loved one so close to the holidays. It's going to make this time of year especially difficult."

I nodded, still bothered and not sure why. Maybe because I was about to release a podcast episode about a man who'd also died from a hit-and-run. Last Christmas Eve. Despite my brain wanting to make some connection, what was factual is someone carelessly or purposefully took these men's lives.

I wondered if Andre was there on the scene. He'd been working on another case most of the weekend. Criminals didn't care about current investigations. Murders happened almost every day.

Hopefully the trail for tonight's victim wouldn't grow cold like it did for Vince Hartman.

Sunday, November 18 at 11:28 p.m.

I curled up in bed with my phone waiting for Andre's nightly call. There was a time where that would've seemed pathetic to do. Waiting on some man to call. Then feeling like an idiot when the call never came.

Thank the Lord, Andre was different.

My phone pinged and I looked down to see I had several Instagram notifications. This time of night, I should have been ignoring social media, but I opened the app anyway. Even though I hadn't put out an episode in months, I gained new followers each week. Tonight, I had two new followers.

I recognized both of them.

Sophia Carlson.

Allison Hartman.

That wasn't surprising since I'd met both earlier today at Greater Zion. I wasn't too sure if it was a good idea for Allison to be following my podcast though. She was a teenager and I wondered if her mother knew she had a social media presence. On further examination, both had also sent me DMs.

I decided to see what the older woman had to say first.

Hi Joss, it's Sophia Carlson. We met earlier today. I think you're doing a wonderful service with your podcast. I know I seemed hesitant earlier, but I did want you to know a lot of people love and miss Vince, especially in the choir. Please be careful with his legacy is all I ask. I hope to see you around at Sugar Creek Café. We'd love to have you back at Greater Zion. Be Blessed, Sister!

I wasn't sure what to think of Sophia's DM. Was it a warning of some sort? From my conversations with others, Vince had a bit of a reputation long before his death. Why was Sophia so resistant to speak about Vince on the podcast? She obviously admired him. Before clicking to read Allison's DM, I decided to peruse Sophia's profile. It was kind of what I expected.

Like most of the people on social media, Sophia loved selfies. She was a pretty woman in her own way. There wasn't a single photo where she wasn't made up, her hairstyle in order and her clothes fashionable. I couldn't tell what Sophia did for a living, but with Grant Carlson as her husband, I had no doubt that she lived well.

There were photos of what had to be the Carlson home. There were a lot of gray and white accents, some natural wood tones. The Carlson's house was lavish, but without any coziness you'd expect in a home. From what I could see, the couple didn't have children, but owned two Pomeranians. With doggy beds in hues of pink and yellow, a plush rug and an assortment of toys organized in baskets, the dogs seemed to have the most colorful room in the house.

Scrolling further back, when the weather was warmer, the Carlsons vacationed on some beach in an exotic location. They were indeed a gorgeous couple.

I stopped scrolling when I found photos with the Hartmans. These had to be at least four years old, taken when Vince and Marianne were married. I really hoped Sophia would be willing to talk. She'd been friendly with Lily despite her obvious allegiance to Marianne. Was she reaching out to Lily more for show? I wondered if the woman was genuinely concerned about Lily or just wanting to see if she'd suffered since Vince's death. Some people could be tricky, giving the appearance of warmth and understanding, when really they were just putting up a facade to gather information.

Before I clicked over to my DMs to see what Allison sent me, I checked her profile.

Private.

I actually was relieved that the young girl didn't have her posts public. I hoped her mother monitored her social media.

I clicked over to the DM and started reading.

My heart dropped.

> Hi Joss - this is Allie. I met you earlier today at church. Sorry about that mess btw. I was just so angry seeing Lily. I never understood what my dad saw in her. But for real, I NEED to talk to you about my dad. Mom's gonna flip when she finds out I messaged you, but there's stuff about my dad that I never told anyone. It might help your investigation. I want to KNOW WHAT HAPPENED TO HIM!

Allison's desperation triggered the little girl in myself who also missed her dad. I guess if I were in her shoes, I'd probably do the same. Unfortunately, she was too young for me to interview on the podcast. And I had a pretty good impression that Marianne would never allow her daughter near me.

Monday, November 18 at 12:10 a.m.

I swiped out of the app and jerked when I realized it was after midnight. I hadn't seen Andre in a few days, but we'd talked. With it being early Monday morning, a whole day had gone by without any communication.

Was he at the scene earlier that I saw on the news? I knew if I didn't get a call from him, he was busy on a case or... or something bad had happened.

Oh, stop it, girl!

I was starting to drive myself crazy with these anxious thoughts. They seemed to have gotten worse with me second-guessing and overthinking everything.

Hold every thought captive.

The phone vibrated in my hand. Late at night, I kept the ringer off. Without even realizing it, I let out a sigh of relief when I saw Andre's name on my caller ID.

"Andre." I squeaked out.

"Hey, babe. I know it's late."

Not wanting him to think he'd woken me up or upset me, I hurriedly said. "You know you can call anytime."

"You need your rest." He admonished in a weary voice, even deeper than usual. "Tomorrow is the big day."

"Oh, yeah. You mean later this morning."

As if sensing my mood shift, Andre's voice sounded tense. "Oh, yeah. Hey, I can see if I can take some time off to come with you."

"There's no need. My grandmother contacted Ms. Eugeena who then promptly reached out to Leesa. It just so happens Leesa is off tomorrow and she will pick me up in the morning. Seems like a lot of trouble. I can drive myself to the courthouse."

"No. I'm glad Leesa can go with you. Everything should be fine, but sometimes it can be emotional. I'm really sorry we haven't been able to spend any quality time together. I miss you."

A smile spread across my face that I wished he could see. "I miss you too, Andre. Are you still working on the same case?"

"Actually, we caught the perp, which is why the chief sent me and Beckett off to another case. Crime never sleeps."

"Oh, I saw on the news earlier about a hit-and-run. Would that be the case?"

Andre didn't respond immediately. "Good guess. That one is... a tough one. They all are, but we got an ID on the victim and notified the next-of-kin."

"That had to be hard." I pressed gently.

Another pause. "It was really emotional," he finally admitted. "Having to tell the loved ones... it never gets easier."

I could hear the weight in his voice, the toll these cases took on him. "I'm sorry," I said softly. "I shouldn't have asked."

"No, it's okay," Andre reassured me. "You're going to find out soon enough. The young man who was killed has been identified as Khalil Rogers."

I frowned. "I'm not sure why his name sounds familiar to me."

Andre commented. "We met him briefly at Carlson Auto. Remember the first salesman that approached us? He went by the name KJ."

I sat up in the bed, an eerie feeling settling over me. "Oh no. That's horrible."

"I know. The family had been expecting him for a surprise birthday party. His birthday. Instead, they got me and Beckett showing up at their door."

Andre didn't often share this much about a case. I know it must have shaken him up since we'd briefly met the victim.

I'd also seen the man at Greater Zion sitting with his co-worker, Terrell Hartman, a little over twelve hours ago. From my brief encounter, he seemed like a nice man.

Was it a horrible accident or something more sinister? A nagging feeling made me lean toward the latter.

Chapter 8

Moving Forward

Monday, November 18 at 8:30 a.m.

I didn't sleep well. The red numbers on the clock appeared blurry and then sharpened as I realized I was no longer sleeping. Thoughts tumbled around in my sleep-deprived brain.

Would I mess up at the grand jury?

Why didn't Sophia want to talk about Vince?

What did Lily miss that last time she saw her husband?

Who hit KJ and left him to die?

Was Vince's death connected?

I needed my mind to focus. I had a long day ahead of me. I slipped out of bed and prayed. When I lifted my head from my clasped hands, Minnie, who liked to sleep on the bed with me, opened one hazel eye. The cat flipped over to show off her white furry belly.

I reached over and rubbed her warm tummy. "I'm glad one of us is enjoying the bed."

The shower helped energize me only slightly. I shuffled over to my closet to figure out what to wear. Most days I wore my café uniform, so picking out clothes on a weekday wasn't easy.

My taste in clothes was eclectic, but I kept clothes that my mother would approve of in the back of my closest. The dark gray suit I chose was actually one my mother insisted I wear during a job hunting phase. After preening in front of the mirror, I studied my reflection. The image that the jurors would see. "You got this, girl."

My grandmother was already up at the kitchen table. "My, my, don't you look businesslike today."

I grinned. "I figured my usual attire wouldn't be appropriate."

Louise frowned, "I love the way you dress. You don't mind expressing yourself. But I agree, being boring works for today's situation. Get you some coffee and one of those muffins."

I wasn't sure I could handle any food, but I chugged down both before I heard a car horn outside. "That's probably Leesa."

Louise shuffled over to me. "You're going to do fine, hon. God's got you. He will make sure that man stays put away for a long time."

I bent down and kissed her. "Thank you."

Leesa drove a minivan and when I opened the passenger door, I was reminded she was the mother of two young kids. The back seat had a car seat for a toddler and a booster seat for her daughter.

Leesa pointed. "Is that your new car? It's so you!"

My RAV4 glinted in the sunlight. "Yep, that's my new girl. I love it." I slid into the minivan's passenger seat and closed the door. "Hey, I really appreciate this. I know you had to have plans for today."

Leesa shook her head. "Nope. I'm good, girl! Chris took the kids to school, so I got a chance to sleep in a bit. And, I got a surprise notification this morning. You didn't tell me you started up the podcast again."

I grimaced. "Yeah, that just happened. I need to catch you up." Anxiety churned in my stomach as I rubbed my clammy hands on my lap. My heart was racing, and I wished the nervousness was only about the episode release, but my brain had no room for that and the people I was about to face.

Leesa chatted, easily navigating the morning traffic. "It was a crazy weekend. Did you hear about the hit and run?"

"Yes, I saw the news last night." Knowing that Andre had revealed the name to me, I kept quiet about that. Although Leesa might already know. Her husband, Chris worked with Andre in homicide. I wondered if Leesa would make any connection to the podcast based on the hit and run elements.

Leesa's voice dropped to a solemn tone. "They announced the guy on the morning news. I was shocked to hear it was Khalil Rogers."

So, Andre was right. Everyone would know the name soon enough. I glanced at Leesa. "Did you know him?"

Leesa glanced at me. "Not that well. I knew of him in high school. He was a few grades ahead of me and..."

Her hesitancy moved my attention away from the fact that we were heading to the courthouse. "And what?"

Leesa shook her head. "Nothing. He used to hang out with Keisha's dad. That's all. You know I try not to think of him."

"Oh, I see." Leesa's daughter, her oldest child, was born when Leesa was still in high school. I was used to Chris Black being the father figure in Keisha's life.

"KJ was a really handsome guy. All the girls liked being around him, of course. He could sing too. You may know him. I've seen him, I think, at Friday Night Jams. Don't you coordinate all the acts that perform?"

Maybe that's where I'd seen him before. I knew his face looked familiar. "I do. Was he a singer or a part of a band?"

Leesa scrunched her nose as if trying to remember. "You know, Briana might know if he was in a band. I do recall him covering a few oldies. He was similar in complexion to Andre, and he had dreadlocks from what I recall."

As Leesa described the man, I could almost see him in my mind. "Yes, he worked at Carlson Auto. He was almost my salesperson."

Leesa exclaimed, "Really? You'll have to tell me about the new car when this is over."

Leesa turned onto Meeting Street. The Charleston Courthouse loomed.

She asked, "Do you want me to stay with you? If so, I can park in the parking garage."

I almost wished I could see a friendly face. "Outside visitors aren't allowed in the grand jury. And I would hate for you to be sitting around for hours."

Leesa fretted as she pulled into a space for me to jump out. "Are you sure? I hate to just drop you off and leave."

"Don't worry! I'll be fine."

She reached over and squeezed my hand. "Text or call me as soon as it's done. I will be right here."

"Thank you, Leesa. I appreciate you." My fingers decided they didn't want to work, so it took me some effort to unbuckle the seatbelt. I waved to Leesa before heading into the court-house.

Monday, November 18 at 9:57 a.m.

I'd been inside the courthouse once when I was called for jury duty a few years ago. Neither side was impressed enough to keep me as a juror. The Charleston Courthouse was grand and a bit intimidating. I entered through security fairly quickly and was directed down a long hallway to the grand jury room.

I paused in the doorway, struck by how different it was from what I'd imagined. Instead of a formal courtroom, I entered a large, windowless conference room with fluorescent lighting that cast a harsh glow over everything. In the center of the room was a long, U-shaped table where the grand jurors, an even mix of men and women, ranging from their late 20s to what looked like early 70s, sat. Their faces were a blend of curiosity and seriousness as they regarded me.

Chief Prosecutor Rutledge approached me.

"Good morning, Ms. Miller. I hope you had a pleasant weekend. Are you ready to get started?"

My mouth felt incredibly dry all of a sudden so I nodded, hoping that I wouldn't embarrass myself. I followed the prosecutor into the room. Like Andre mentioned last week, there was no defense attorney or judge present. A clerk sat in the corner, ready to record the proceedings.

I sat in a chair facing the grand jury, feeling exposed under their collective gaze. The room seemed to shrink around me as the prosecutor smiled at me. I think he was trying to put me at ease, but underneath the table I twisted my anxious fingers.

"Ms. Miller," he began, his voice echoing slightly in the quiet room. "Can you please tell us about your interactions with the defendant Caleb Davenport?"

I took a deep breath, acutely aware of every eye on me. The room didn't feel warm when I first walked in, but I felt sweat beading on my forehead as I spoke. A glass of water sat in front of me.

Was that there before?

Grateful, I took a small sip before responding. "I met him at the café where I worked. I knew him by another name... Liam."

"When did you first suspect something was amiss?"

I frowned. "Well, I didn't. I'd been interviewing people who knew the artist Rebecca Montgomery. Looking back, it did seem like he was always around, but I assumed that was because of his social media presence. He was a big influencer who built his platform off getting stories. It was only later that... that I realized he'd developed a bit of an obsession, much like the one with Rebecca Montgomery."

Rutledge cleared his throat. "We do want to stick to the events that happened to you, Ms. Miller. Can you describe what occurred the night of July 8th?"

Here is what I dreaded, forcing myself to relive those moments. They popped into my head when I didn't want them to, while I slept or while I was under a lot of stress.

I took another sip of water.

Rutledge smiled at me. "Take your time, Ms. Miller."

I described finding my car unable to start, forcing me to return back inside the café. As I talked, the jurors seemed to disappear as I went back in time describing the broken back door and knowing I was not alone.

"I was trying to escape toward the front of the café when my... when Detective Andre Baez arrived. His partner, Detective Grayson Beckett headed around back and stopped Caleb."

The questioning continued for another half an hour. The jurors were curious about my episodes into Rebecca's disappearance. Some jurors leaned forward, clearly engrossed in my responses. Others maintained poker faces, probably ready for this to be over with like me. One elderly man in the back row seemed to be fighting to stay awake.

At some point, my nervousness had fallen away, and I believed the jurors would ensure Caleb stood trial. When we adjourned, I had to keep myself from sprinting from the courtroom. Once outside the heavy doors, I took a deep breath.

I was surprised to see Leesa bounce up from a bench.

"Have you been waiting all this time?"

"I've only been here a few minutes. I wasn't going to leave you hanging, girl. She peered into my eyes, her face anxious. "How do you feel?"

I exhaled deeply. "I did it. Hopefully I can move forward."

Leesa's eyes widened. "You may not have a choice. You have got to read some of these comments on social media. The episode you dropped this morning has blown up."

I groaned. *What had I done?*

Monday, November 18 at 9:39 p.m.

As expected, a storm of comments showered around Lily's interview. I had no intentions of facing the debris on a hungry stomach, so I insisted on taking Leesa to lunch. We stopped by a neighborhood favorite, The Chicken Shack. Comfort food sounded like a balm for the soul. Never mind that I'd had fried chicken yesterday at Greater Zion, as Leesa filled me in, I devoured my two piece chicken meal which included a side of mashed potatoes and gravy and a honey-flavored biscuit.

Leesa slurped her lemonade before continuing. "Apparently, folks still feel like Vince and Lily got married too quickly. Here is one." She flipped her phone to where she had zoomed in on a comment.

> @ChurchChoirMom: "Remember how they got married so quickly. Always thought there was more to that story. That girl probably got a lot of insurance money off Vince."

Leesa shook her head. "There are tons of these."

I sighed and wiped my fingers on a napkin, adding to the pile already surrounding my plate. Before I opened Instagram, I saw I had a few phone messages and voicemails as well. I decided to tackle the social media comments head on first. My eyes widened as I saw over 100 comments under the post.

For these new episodes, I planned to include a clip from the show with a graphic. I'd chosen to feature Lily saying, "I've been learning to cope and appreciate the short time that we had together."

I thought it was a good safe clip, but most posters had something to say.

> @TLuv1973: Why is Lily doing interviews now? She just trying to get attention again. #AttentionSeeker

> @Queen91: Poor Vince. His ex-wife must be furious hearing Lily talk about their marriage like this.

> @DivaLex843: Lily needs to let sleeping dogs lie. Bringing all this up again is just hurting Vince's family. #MoveOn

> @ColdCaseEnthusiast: Does anyone else think Lily might be hiding something? Her

story seems too convenient. Do they have proof that she didn't go after her husband?

@Precious1998: Vince was such a respected member of our community. Sad to see his memory dragged through the mud like this.

@TrueCrimeFanatic: I bet there's way more to this story than Lily's letting on. Can't wait to hear what others have to say!

My stomach knotted and not because the food was bad. "These comments are brutal. I need to check on Lily. This might have been a mistake."

Leesa curled her lips in disgust. "Girl, most of those comments probably came from people at that church. It's a shame, but people use social media to hide their ugliness."

I agreed. But I let this ball start and I felt responsible. I could take everything down, but that wouldn't look good for me trying to build a reputation as a true crime podcaster.

My phone lit up again. My heart leaped. Lily?

No, it wasn't her.

"Oh no," I groaned.

Leesa sucked in a breath. "What's wrong? Did something happen?"

I flipped my phone around so Leesa could see the image on the screen.

Leesa's eyes widened. "Oooh, girl."

I grimaced as I answered the phone, tightening my body from the oncoming tongue lashing. "Hello, Mom."

Mom huffed into the phone. "Jocelyn Marie Miller, where are you?"

I closed my eyes as my mother dragged out my whole government name.

My head started to throb. I had a feeling this day was only going to get worse.

Monday, November 18 at 1:16 p.m.

Leesa and I were quiet on the drive back home. I appreciated how my friend understood mother-daughter dynamics. My mom and I were a lot closer when I was younger. Until, like most teenagers, I rebelled and wanted to be my own woman.

We really drifted apart after my dad died. That's when I realized how much of a daddy's girl I'd been. Both my brother and I were young adults trying to learn who we were without our parents. Then one of them permanently left forever, and Mom, she kind of buried herself in her work.

She didn't get to enjoy the empty nest phase with her best friend beside her. That, along with losing her adoptive parents and dealing with how she'd been born into this world, left Clarice Miller as one very complicated woman.

But I loved my mother. Unlike my brother, who'd traipsed around living his own life, I stayed in Sugar Creek and tried to be a dutiful daughter. And I'd learned that the way my mother showed care often sounded more like criticism, which made for awkward conversations. We were both adults and I would have liked to have a relationship by now where I considered my mom a friend.

When Leesa pulled up in front of Louise's house, I audibly gasped like I was a child who'd been caught being bad. I'd planned to drive over to the home where I grew up, but Mom's Toyota Sienna sat in the driveway waiting for me. I'd clearly underestimated how upset Clarice Miller was. My mom rarely came to her biological mother's house. While I'd embraced Louise, my mom tiptoed around that relationship. Mother-daughter dynamics were incredibly dysfunctional in my family.

I glanced at Leesa. "Thank you again."

Leesa smiled. "You know I got you, girl." Her smile wavered as she peered apprehensively through the passenger window. "Is that your mother's car?"

I nodded and held my clutched hands up in a prayer position.

Leesa's eyebrows shot up. "I'm going to pray for you. Just remember your mama loves you in her own way. I had to learn that about Eugeena Patterson."

I chuckled, grateful for the release since what I was about to walk into was no laughing matter. I climbed out of Leesa's minivan and braced myself. The walk up the driveway felt like a slow motion effect. If Louise and my mother were in the living room, I had no doubt they were watching my approach through the bay windows. When I opened the front door, I could feel the awkward tension in the living room.

Louise grinned at me, but her smile wasn't its usual brightness. "Joss, look who came by to visit."

I cringed. I knew Louise longed to have more contact with the biological daughter she'd been forced to give up. "Hey, Mom. I could have come to see you."

My mother waved like it was no big deal, but there was strain on her face. Mom was a typical introvert who didn't enjoy small talk. "I closed up the office and figured coming to Louise's house was closer."

Mom owned her own accounting business. She often started her office hours early in the morning or worked into the wee hours of the evening. But she was always available when we needed her. Today, she'd made it a point to find me.

Slowly, Louise stood from her chair. "Well, I'm going to head next door to Eugeena's. I will give you and your mama some time to talk."

I frowned. This was Louise's house. "You don't need to leave."

Louise jabbed a finger in my direction, her voice stern. "Talk to your mama. You should keep her in the loop, so she doesn't worry about you."

I stepped back, a bit surprised. I was an adult, and Louise rarely scolded me about anything. Now I wondered what she and my mom talked about before I arrived.

We both watched Louise shuffle out the door, closing it softly behind her. It dawned on me that I hadn't told my mom a lot of things. I guess she had a right to be furious with me. Mom was understandably still upset about me being attacked last summer, often wondering aloud why I still worked at the café.

I loved working at the café before everything went down.

Most days, I still enjoyed being at the café. But there were days when my mind didn't want to cooperate, bringing up memories that sucked me back into that night.

I sank down in Louise's vacated chair. "I'm sorry."

Mom asked sharply, "About what? The fact that you testified at a grand jury hearing this morning or that you started that podcast up again? Isn't that how you got into trouble in the first place?"

I bowed my head, unable to look at my mother. Testifying this morning had taken a lot more out of me than I realized. "The grand jury came up quickly. A lot happened last week. I got a new car and..."

Why was I making excuses?

I knew by now I needed to reach out to my mom. She wasn't going to reach out to me. She lived her life and I lived mine. Our way of existing only became a problem when she found out things that I should have told her.

"Well, I hope things went well for you. They need to get that man sentenced and permanently behind bars." Mom twisted her fingers in her lap. "Which makes no sense why you're digging into another case. That crazy man went after you."

"This is different," I croaked, not believing my own words.

"Is it?" My mother's voice rose an octave. "They're saying Vince Hartman's car wreck was no accident since the driver left the scene. Suppose it was on purpose. The person responsible is still driving around."

I nodded, knowing opening my mouth wouldn't help. When I was younger, I learned talking back and expressing my opinion to my mom was a big mistake.

Mom stood from the couch and paced. "I know Andre had to say something to you about this. What did he say?"

My mom liked Andre, which was a good thing. She didn't care for most of my past boyfriends. "He's not that happy about it either, but he told me to keep him updated on anything weird. And I will. I know I'm not an expert. My podcast still focuses on those who loved the victim having an opportunity to tell their story."

Mom pursed her lips, placing her hands on her hips. "Well, you tell Andre I'm disappointed in him. I can't believe he's supporting you with this mess. You know if your father was..."

I looked up at her, surprised she would start a statement like that.

She rarely talked about my father.

As if she shocked herself, she stopped pacing abruptly, giving me a wide-eyed look. Then she sat down, steepling her hands under her chin. "What am I saying? He would have encouraged you. Probably would have helped you. You're just like him. Your father always loved a mystery."

My nose grew warm, which started a domino effect. In a matter of seconds, tears welled up in my eyes. I hadn't thought about that similarity with my dad until my mom mentioned it. He loved reading James Patterson and Walter Mosley. We would watch all the *Law and Order*, *CSI* and *NCIS* shows.

An uncomfortable silence settled over both of us. Ginger, who'd been napping someplace in the living room, took that moment to walk into the middle of the living room floor and began grooming himself.

Mom stared at the cat and blinked. "Louise has cats."

"She has three cats. Minnie and Mickey are around here someplace."

"Oh." Mom said still looking at the big orange cat. "He kind of looks like Garfield."

I laughed. "Yes, he does." I cleared my throat, hoping to change the direction of the conversation. "How did you find out about the grand jury hearing this morning?"

Turning her attention from the cat, my mother focused her eyes on me. "I called you. Twice. I kept getting your voicemail.

So, I thought maybe you were busy at the café. Fay told me where you were today. Everyone seemed to know but me."

I rubbed my head, a headache had started to stir when I answered my mom's call. Now my head throbbed. "What did you need?"

Mom looked away. "I wanted to ask if you've heard from your brother?"

I frowned. "No, I haven't heard from him in a few months. Why?"

"I wondered if he knew... if he'd heard about Khalil."

My brow furrowed. "Khalil Rogers? Nate knew him?"

Mom tilted her head. "Yes, they hung out all the time. You might remember him by his nickname. KJ."

KJ knew my brother.

How did I forget that?

Then again, Nate seemed to always have a huge posse of friends. He was a jock, playing football and basketball. When it appeared he wasn't good enough to further his career in either sport, he became more sullen. Increasingly distant, even before Dad got sick.

Mom shook her head. "It's such a shame. He's only been married a few years and they have a little girl. Marianne Hartman called and told me about him. Danvers has the body. They will do his funeral. She was really broken up about him. Apparently, he was her godson, one of Marianne's best friend's sons. When her friend died, KJ stayed with them for a year until he graduated high school."

My ears perked up. "Were Marianne and Vince still married then?"

Mom nodded. "Oh, yes. This would have been early in their marriage when their daughter Allison was still young."

That meant KJ and Vince knew each other. Something nipped at my mind. Last night I'd pondered if the hit and runs were a coincidence. Now I wondered if they could be connected? Since my mom seemed to have cooled down, I asked. "What did you think of Vince?"

My mother shrugged. "I only met him a few times. Marianne handled their business affairs and their taxes. She also runs her family's funeral home. She said her husband didn't like to deal with any of that stuff."

"Vince couldn't have made much of an income as a choir director? What else did he do?"

"I'm not gossiping about my clients," Mom started, but then she gave me a look.

"What? This wouldn't go farther than this room. I promise."

Mom sighed. "Vince didn't keep a steady job. During the time he was married to Marianne, he worked at the funeral home for a while. Then him and his brother started a business. It barely lasted two years. The last few years of their marriage, he worked at Crescendo Music Academy."

"Sounds like that was a perfect fit for him." I knew about stumbling around trying to find out what you wanted to be when you grew up. One thing I knew I didn't want to be was an accountant like my parents. I even toyed with going to nursing school. Working as a barista wasn't a career goal, but I enjoyed it.

The more I learned about Vince, he didn't seem all that complicated. People got divorced all the time, and sometimes it took you awhile to find a career. Lily said their relationship came after the divorce. But with his new marriage, it sounded like quite a few people were upset.

That got me wondering about whoever slammed into Vince's car. Was it truly random? It's possible a drunk driver could have done it and forgot what happened. That would be vehicular manslaughter. But if someone followed him and purposely ran him off the road, that was murder.

What could a choir director have done to cause someone to want to hurt him?

"It's weird that KJ was run down with a car almost a year after Vince's car was hit and run off the road. And they knew each other."

My mother shook her head as she glared at me. "What are you doing? You're investigating? You're no detective. You work at a coffee shop, Joss."

I massaged my temples. My mom spoke about my choice of employment as if it was a bad thing. "I love my job. Anyway, I kicked off this first episode and people are going to want to know more. I'm not the only one who's curious. You know Marianne. I'm sure she and her daughter need closure too."

My mom's shoulders slumped. "I told Marianne this was all harmless."

I edged to the front of the chair. "What do you mean?" Then it hit me. "Wait, she called you?"

Mom looked at me. "She was concerned about you wanting to talk to Allison. Marianne is protective of her daughter, even more so after the divorce."

Stuck on what my mom said, I started to seethe. "I didn't reach out to Allison. She reached out to me. I know she's a minor and I can't interview her."

Mom gazed into my eyes, her face stony. "Good. Joss, you don't want to get tangled up with Marianne Hartman. She sounded plenty annoyed that Lily put her business out there. Lily is much younger, she's your age. I guess it seems like nothing to tell your business to people on social media. But some of us are old school. We like our privacy."

Mom stood from the couch. "I need to go. Louise has been kind enough to give us her home to talk. Tell her I said thank you."

I walked Mom out onto the front porch and glanced next door. Louise and Ms. Eugeena sat on her porch. They both waved at us. We waved back with smiles on our faces. But there was nothing pleasant about my smile. If anything, I was disturbed.

My mom turned around and looked at me, her face softer. "I know we go long periods of time without talking to each other. That's my fault. I worry about your brother all the time. He never calls. But you, I'm glad you're at least close by. I am your mother. I would like to be there for you."

She didn't reach for me, but I reached out and grabbed her hand.

My stoic mom teared up and squeezed my hand. "Joss, please be careful." And with that, she let go of my hand and marched over to her car.

Even though my mom's visit resulted in her scolding me, I couldn't help but think it had also been fruitful on a number of fronts.

Later that night, after talking to Andre, I read through the posts about KJ. I remembered him more clearly coming to the house with my brother. He didn't have the dreadlocks back then and was one of the quieter members of my brother's tribe. Did Nate even stay in touch with any of those guys?

I scrolled through my text messages I'd sent to my brother. Some received no responses. Other times, Nate's responses were sterile, like I was a stranger.

I clicked the share button on the news article about KJ's death. Then I typed a message:

> **"Hey, Nate, thought you should know KJ was killed. Here's the article."**

I hit send.

That was a bit harsh. Maybe this would be the thing to break through the wall of silence between us. Nate was like my mother. He wasn't one to reach out.

Hopefully, this would get his attention.

Chapter 9

Tensions Rising

Tuesday, November 19 at 5:55 p.m.

I washed and then rinsed the carafe in the kitchen. Before returning back up front, I paused, my eyes fixated on the back door. It was locked tight. Briana had taken out the trash earlier. I hadn't gone out back in months. I flashed back to that night when I realized I wasn't alone.

A figure in the dark.

"Joss, are you okay?"

Startled, I jumped to see Fay watching me from her office door, her face concerned.

"I'm good!" My voice sounded false in my own ears. One of these days, that night would become a distant memory and it wouldn't bother me anymore.

At least, that was my constant prayer. I knew God heard me. I was here, alive and still working at the café.

"Joss, are you sure?" Fay stepped away from the office door and moved closer toward me. "It's okay if you're not."

I audibly sighed letting out a breath I didn't realize I'd been holding. Fay was always inquiring about my state of mind. I appreciated her so much, but I'd grown weary with the concern too.

I wanted, needed, things to go back to the way it was before.

I guess I wasn't helping by standing in the middle of the kitchen staring at the back door.

"I will be okay." My voice firm. "Look, I'm going to finish cleaning up front." I had no trouble grinning. "Eleanor is the only one left in the café as usual."

Fay smiled back. "Of course. We should post a sign over that booth, Eleanor's Office. But I can't complain, she is a fabulous customer. I saw she even included Sugar Creek Café in her acknowledgements."

I raised an eyebrow. "You've been reading her books?"

Fay rolled her eyes. "Um, yeah. I need to know if she's writing about us and our customers."

That made me laugh out loud. Writers do like to write about what they observe around them. I headed up front. My tired feet dragged a bit, but it felt good to be back. Yesterday held way too much drama for me. Andre had a good laugh when I told him about my mother dropping by to scold me. I still felt like it was no laughing matter, but I took my mom reaching out for a change as a good thing. Too bad Marianne Hartman's call instigated it.

I'd checked my messages throughout the day and hadn't heard from Marianne or Allison Hartman. My mother had me slightly scared about Marianne, which kind of made me a bit curious too. I wanted to know what Marianne had to say about Vince, to compare her opinion to Lily's. Marianne had been married to him a whole lot longer.

Eleanor walked over to the counter with her laptop bag on her shoulder. "Joss, dear, I just finished listening to your new episode. You're really getting the hang of this true crime investigating business."

I flushed. "Thanks, Eleanor. I'm not sure I'd call myself an investigator, though. And certain people in my life think I'm making a mistake."

Eleanor waved her hand dismissively. "Nonsense. You have a natural talent for setting interviewees at ease."

"I appreciate your feedback. It means a lot coming from our resident mystery author."

Eleanor winked. "You have your own detective too. Does that help?"

I laughed. "Sure, Andre doesn't mind giving his opinion. And he listens to my most recent episodes before I publish them to the world."

"That's a good collaboration." Eleanor mused.

I agreed. "We are quite the pair. Sometimes him being a homicide detective makes me nervous, but my amateur sleuthing makes him equally uncomfortable."

"I'd say you two balance each other out. You're there for him and he for you. I need to head on home. Those kitties are ready to be fed. Have a good evening."

"You too, Eleanor."

As Eleanor walked out, I glanced over and noticed the lights were on in the center. Briana walked through the connecting doors into the café, her face solemn.

"What's going on over there?" I asked. Not being in the café yesterday, I must have missed something.

"Oh, Indigo Soul needed a place to practice," Briana explained. "Even though the center isn't officially open yet, Fay gave us the okay to test out the acoustics since we will be in there for Friday Night Jams."

It had been such a long week and it was only Tuesday. I'd almost forgotten about Friday Night Jam. Fay let me plan two jams a month now. One every first Friday and the other on the third Friday. In the new year, the center would officially open with classes and community events, but Fay decided it was okay to move Friday Night Jams from the café. The jams had been pretty packed for a while, nearing the maximum number of people allowed for our building code regulations.

Briana leaned on the counter. "It's a weird time for us though. I'm not sure how everyone is going to feel about doing the jam on Friday."

"Why?" I inquired.

"They're processing Khalil's death. We all called him KJ," Briana said. "Anyway, he was one of the founding members of the band with Jake. Did you know him?"

"My mother reminded me that KJ hung out with my brother. I hadn't seen him in years. Then, Andre and I ran into him last week at Carlson Auto. He was the first salesperson who inquired about helping us before Terrell stepped in."

Briana wrinkled her nose. "Really? KJ was a cool guy." She tilted her head. "Your brother knew him, huh. Where is your brother? All these years, and I've never met him."

My heart felt a pang. "Good question. It's been awhile since my brother has been in Sugar Creek."

Briana nodded. "I get it. It's a bit of a pain getting along with siblings sometimes. You know my sister is in Seattle, but she does try to make it to the East Coast when she can." She glanced back toward the art center's entrance, then turned to me. "So have you met everyone in the band?"

"I've seen them perform at past Friday Night Jams. I'm glad you were able to get them to come back. You all are big time now! Almost too big for Sugar Creek Café jams."

Briana threw her head back and laughed. "Those guys love being on the road, but I told them it's good to play in our own backyard sometimes too. Why don't you come meet them?" Briana raised an eyebrow, her voice low. "I'm sure you want to see who Lily walked away from."

"Absolutely."

I traipsed behind Briana next door into the center. I was definitely interested in meeting the male lead singer and Lily's former boyfriend up close. I'd been doing my research. Social media was helpful with this since most people posted photos.

As we entered, I recognized Jake Reaves right away. I'd seen him plenty of times at Friday Night Jam, but had never really chatted with him. He was tall and lean with deep brown skin that seemed to glow under the lights. His dreadlocks were pulled back into a ponytail, a few escaping to frame his face. Longer fingers danced across the guitar strings with a familiar tune that I couldn't recall.

I could immediately tell he was different from Vince Hart-man. He was a lot closer in age to Lily compared to Vince who had been in his late forties. Jake wore his jeans low around his hips, and despite the cooler temperatures, he wore a tight black t-shirt that accentuated the physique of a man who liked to work out.

To Jake's left was another guitarist, but his guitar hung off his shoulders as he watched Jake play. His curly hair was wrapped into a man bun. Behind them, a drummer tapped softly on the drums. On the far right, a guy played a few keys on the keyboard. I assumed maybe they were warming up for practice.

I whispered to Briana, who continued to approach. "Is this a good time to be doing introductions?"

Briana glanced at me. "They're kind of in limbo right now. We may not get much done tonight with practice." She turned and waved. "Hey, guys, you probably know Joss."

They all looked in our direction as we approached, their eyes solemn.

Briana stepped forward, gesturing to each band member in turn. "Joss, this is Jake on lead vocals and guitar, Phil on lead guitar, Devonté on drums, and Ricky on keyboard."

The guys nodded and waved a greeting.

I clasped my hands together in front of me. "It's nice to meet you all. It's been awhile since we had you all perform at Friday Night Jams."

Jake stepped off the small stage. "Absolutely. This center is amazing. You guys are going to have a lot of bands who want to get inside here." He turned around. "I really like the classroom setups. I'm excited for our next generation of young creatives."

I smiled. "We definitely intend to use it for what the center was named for, teaching young people all about the arts."

"That's fantastic! They sure don't get that education in public schools anymore." Jake's face broke into a wide grin as he set his guitar aside. "Joss... What's your last name? I feel like I know you from someplace else."

"Well, I work as a barista at the café too. But my last name is Miller. Joss Miller."

Jake's eyebrows shot up as he stepped forward. "Miller? Wait. Are you related to Nate Miller?"

I nodded, surprised. "You know my brother?"

Jake's face softened. "Yeah, now I know where I've seen you. I knew you coordinated Friday Night Jams for the café, but I remember seeing you back in school too. Where is Nate these days?"

Yet another mention of my absentee brother, who still hadn't returned my text. I grimaced. "He lives in Atlanta. He doesn't come back to Sugar Creek a lot."

Jake nodded. "I see. I haven't seen him in years. I think the last time I saw him was at your dad's funeral. We all came to support him."

I felt a lump in my throat. Everything that day and for months after had been a haze. "I'm sorry for your loss," I said. "I understand you all lost a member of the band."

Jake nodded. "KJ. Yeah, me and him started Indigo Soul... along with Lily Foster." Jake closed his eyes. When he opened them there was a mixture of pain and sadness. "Sorry, she goes by Lily Hartman these days."

An awkward silence settled over the big room. The band members behind Jake seemed to be tuning their instruments. I glanced at Briana, who pursed her lips.

Briana piped up. "You know Joss is also a podcaster too."

Jake's eyes sharpened on me. "So, you're the one doing the story on Vince Hartman?"

I nodded and raised my arm. "That's me."

"I listened to your episode with Lily," Jake said, his expression unreadable. "It's... good to see her coming back to herself. "

"Yes, not having closure is hard."

Jake's expression tightened. "I will never understand what Lily saw in Vince. He didn't deserve her. Let's just say if a man cheats, he'll always cheat again. There's no telling what other areas in his life he chose to be dishonest."

My heart rate picked up. "Are you saying Vince was cheating with Lily or on Lily?"

Jake's face clouded over. "Vince went out of his way to pursue Lily, you know."

I couldn't help but probe further. "Were you shocked by how quickly Lily moved on?"

Jake's eyes met mine, a mix of pain and suspicion in them. "Something was funny about the whole thing. Lily couldn't have fallen for Vince that fast. It just... it didn't make sense." He paused, then added with a hint of remorse, "But I'm not here to smear Lily's name. We both took a break, that's all. We weren't meant to be. Ancient history."

Before I could ask anything else, Jake shook his head as if clearing away the memories. "Look, I've got to get back to the band. We've got a set to practice. We want to impress the home crowd on Friday and do KJ proud."

Briana looked at me, her eyes apologetic.

I touched her arm. "Enjoy the practice. We can catch up later." I was sure if anything else was said that I needed to know, Briana would share it with me.

I approached the door to the café, startled by the figure standing in the doorway. Lily stood there with her eyes wide staring in the direction of the band.

I didn't have to turn back to know she'd seen Jake.

And I bet he'd noticed her too.

Tuesday, November 19 at 6:16 p.m.

Lily's eyes immediately locked with Jake's from across the room. The tension between them was palpable, crackling through the air like static electricity. I wondered if she came here to see him.

But how did she know he was here?

Lily blinked as if trying to break a trance. She looked at me and then beckoned me over with a quick wave of her hand.

I glanced back at Jake, who sat with his fingers frozen across the guitar strings, staring at Lily. I almost preferred it if Lily was here to see Jake. It was obvious from our brief conversation that the man still loved her.

Had she made a mistake moving on with Vince?

I passed through the door and let it shut behind us before starting. "Look, I'm sorry about all the attention coming from the podcast. I can take it down, but—"

"No!" Lily stated sharply, her face distressed. "This is what we needed. The police stopped looking into what happened to Vince. We need to put as much attention back on his *murder* as possible. I'm not worried about what people are saying. It's old news to me. They've been saying that stuff before I even married Vince."

I held up my hands. "Okay." From my peripheral, I could see movement near the counter. Glancing over, I saw it was Fay with her arms folded.

"Is everything okay?" Fay asked.

Lily smiled at Fay. "It's fine. I know you all are supposed to be closing up, but I wanted to catch Joss."

Fay nodded. "Go ahead. We're going to be here for a while since the band is practicing next door."

Lily looked behind me through the glass door.

I touched her arm. "We can go to the back of the café and sit."

She nodded, following me.

"Are there others who want to talk about Vince?" she asked, her fingers nervously twisting the strap of her purse.

I blew out a breath. "The only person who's reached out is Allison. Then her mother reached out to my mother like I'm twelve or something, warning me away from her daughter."

Lily rolled her eyes. "That's Marianne. Always trying to control things. She's probably pretty upset that you did the interview with me. Allison is not that young."

I protested. "She's a teenager."

"Who will turn eighteen in a month or so. She was born the day after Christmas."

"Oh, wow. I didn't realize she had a birthday close to Christmas. That makes losing her dad even more horrible."

Lily opened her mouth to speak, then closed it again as if reconsidering her words. Finally, she said, "Joss, I'm not sure it's a good idea to talk to either one of them."

"Why not?" I asked. "They were both important parts of Vince's life. Their perspectives will want to be heard too." While I wasn't officially a journalist, I understood I couldn't be biased, only sharing certain sides.

Lily glanced over her shoulder as if she expected someone to come through the doorway. Jake, perhaps.

She turned to me. "I have a few people who would be willing to talk to you. One is Valerie Hartman."

I about choked and I wasn't even drinking anything. "Is she related to Vince?"

"Yes, Valerie is Vince's younger sister. And she absolutely wants to talk to you. Don't worry. Valerie and I are friends. In fact, she's the reason Vince and I got together in the first place."

I nodded. "I remember you mentioning that in the episode."

Lily crossed her arms. "Valerie knew Vince in a way that others didn't. And she knew me before... well, before all these silly rumors."

I pulled my phone from my apron. "Okay, I'll reach out to her. What's the best way to reach her?"

Lily texted me her phone number. "She's also on Instagram all the time, @fiercediva. So you can DM her too. I told her she could reach out to you, which might be better."

I opened my IG app and searched for the handle. A pretty chocolate skinned woman appeared with a body that most women dreamed about. I scrolled quickly down her feed. "Does she work at a gym or something?"

Lily nodded. "Yes, she teaches spin classes. You can tell from her fabulous body."

"I need to take her class." I commented.

Lily reached into her purse and pulled out a business card. "Here is someone else you should talk to as well. Carolyn Becker. She owns Crescendo Music Academy where Vince worked."

I took the card, a question forming in my mind. "Did the police talk to Valerie and Carolyn?"

Lily shook her head. "No. The police focused on me. They even questioned Marianne. And Jake, of course."

I raised my eyebrows. "They looked at people closest to Vince. Spouses. And your ex-boyfriend. Why did they look at Jake?"

Lily's shoulders stiffened. "That was Marianne's doing. She had no business pulling Jake in like that."

I wanted to ask more questions, but Lily stood all of a sudden. "I should go. I really appreciate that you have been willing to take this on. It's been a long time, and while people are fussing, I know everyone wants to know the truth, so we can all move on."

I let Lily out the café door and locked it behind her. I made my way to the counter where Fay was wiping down the espresso machine, her brow furrowed with concern.

It was my turn to ask. "Everything okay?"

Fay looked at me. "I don't know, but this can't be good."

I followed her eyes to where Lily stood outside talking to Jake.

I leaned against the counter. "Does it worry you to see them together like this?"

Fay crossed her arms. "A little. They have so much history, and with everything that's happened, I hope they're not going to complicate things more."

A thought struck me about the couple. Lily came to me wanting to do the podcast and even suggested more people for me to interview. What if neither her or Jake was as innocent as they claimed? What if they were both involved in Vince's death somehow?

Like I told Andre, I wasn't going to take anyone's word at face value.

Chapter 10

Sisterly Love

Tuesday, November 19 at 10:04 p.m.

I checked out Lily's recommendations. While I was excited about having two more interviews, I was weary that Lily seemed to be pushing for the episodes. This was new for me, but I still planned to do my homework so I could write my questions. Social media wasn't always trustworthy, but it's where you learned the most about people. At least what people wanted you to know. I started researching Vince's sister first. I found it hard to believe she would even talk to me, but Lily claimed they were good friends.

I could tell from Valerie's Instagram page, @fiercediva, that she must be the firecracker in the family. She shared the sharp cheekbones and slanted brown eyes that ran in her family. The Hartmans were indeed a beautiful family, a variety of hues from caramel to milk chocolate.

Valerie's clothes were bold and quite sexy, and she wore a pixie cut dyed honey blond. As a fitness instructor, she had the body to make almost anything work. Many of the reels showed Valerie hyping her spin class, her voice commanding over a hip-hop or trap beat. I got so caught up in watching those videos, I forgot I was supposed to be doing research. I made note of when Valerie had classes and decided maybe I should finally join a gym again.

I sent Valerie a DM.

> @coldjusticepodcast: Hi Valerie, I'm Joss Miller from the *Cold Justice* podcast. Lily mentioned you would be willing to be interviewed on the podcast. I'd love to talk to you about your brother Vince. Would you be willing to talk this Wednesday? Happy to meet wherever you're comfortable.

Next I explored Carolyn Becker's Facebook page, the social media platform where she was most active. From the few personal photos I could see, she was married and had three grown children. Her posts were more devoted to her school and students.

I clicked over to the website for Crescendo Music Academy. The website had a clean, elegant design with a large photo of a converted Victorian house on Ashley Avenue where the school operated. I didn't know the music school existed. It blended in with the other residential buildings.

Students of all ages attended for either instrument lessons or voice lessons. Carolyn was a renowned classical pianist, who played in the Charleston Philharmonic. Upon further reading of her bio, I learned she had performed with orchestras and choirs across the world before returning home to Charleston.

So, this is where Vince last worked. It sounded like the perfect place for the Greater Zion choir director. As I scrolled through the faculty page, I was surprised that Vince's photo remained on the site. It was marked with a small "In Memoriam" banner. His warm smile and kind eyes peered back at me from the page. That the dead man had so much life was eerie and sad at the same time.

He must have meant a lot to Carolyn too.

I sent her a friend request on Facebook but then noticed her last post was from two weeks ago. Mrs. Becker struck me as the kind of person who preferred email. I went back to the school's website and found an email on her contact page.

Subject: Inquiry about Vince Hartman - Cold Justice Podcast

Dear Mrs. Becker,

My name is Joss Miller. I host the Cold Justice podcast, where I investigate cold cases in the Charleston area. Lily Hartman may have told you I'm currently working on a story about Vince. I understand he was an important part of the Crescendo Music Academy. Your perspective as his colleague and the founder of Crescendo Music Academy would be invaluable to understanding this part of his story.

I aim to honor Vince's memory and hopefully shed some light on the circumstances surrounding his death. Would you be willing to meet with me to share your memories of working with Vince? I'm usually off on Wednesdays, but can meet on the weekend as well.

I'm happy to meet you at a time and place that's convenient for you.

Thank you for considering my request.

Best regards,

Joss Miller

Host, Cold Justice podcast

By the time I hit send on the email, my phone rang. I smiled when I saw one of my favorite photos appear. I often snapped photos of Andre so I had lots of them to choose from in my photo album. I was by no means a professional photographer, but he had the most photogenic face I knew. I loved the way he grinned when he was well rested and in the kitchen doing what he loved.

I answered the phone. It had been awhile since we'd been together. "Hey, Andre."

"What's up, babe. How was your day?"

I loved to have someone who genuinely asked how I was doing. Even though we'd not been hanging out as much, little things like that made this relationship special. "Well, I have two prospects for interviews about Vince Hartman."

"Already?" Andre sounded surprised.

"I should mention that Lily helped me out. One is Vince's younger sister and the other is his co-worker from the Crescendo Music Academy. I just made contact with them, so the interviews aren't scheduled yet."

Andre asked, "So Lily recruited them for your podcast?"

"Yeah. You don't need to sound so suspicious. She said they were both interested."

I heard a scratching noise through the phone as Andre shifted. "So, this doesn't concern you?"

"Maybe... a little. I mean Lily really wants to know what happened to her husband. It makes sense that other people that knew him want to come forward to talk about him too. And

Lily said the police never talked to either woman. Maybe there's something they noticed."

Andre blew out a breath. "I'm not going to keep sounding like a broken record, but—"

"I know, I know. I will be careful. Enough about me. How was your day?"

Andre didn't respond for a few seconds, so I thought he must have fallen asleep. Then finally he said, "I can't get into it too much, but there are some disturbing details about KJ's case."

Andre's mention of KJ made me realize I'd never heard back from Nate. He was kind of sporadic, sometimes he responded to texts and sometimes it felt like he was ghosting me.

Why was my brother like that and where was he?

"Joss, are you okay?" There was concern etched into Andre's voice.

"Yes, sorry. My mom told me KJ hung out with my brother, but that was years ago. I texted my brother last night and he hasn't responded. I don't know why he's so unresponsive sometimes. It's annoying."

"Maybe he's processing, babe. Does he usually come back to Sugar Creek for the holidays?"

I sighed. "He came last Thanksgiving, but not Christmas." Andre and I had only been dating since the first of this year so Nate wasn't even aware of my current boyfriend.

"Oh, by the way, I met Jake, Lily's ex and the other band members from Indigo Soul. Fay let them practice in the center tonight for the Friday Night Jam coming up. Get this, KJ was one of the founding members."

"Really? Small world."

"That's Sugar Creek for you. So, I know you can't talk about it, but is there anything that people should be concerned about. Like, was KJ targeted?"

My mind went to Vince's death again, even though his murder happened a year ago.

"I would say that KJ could have made an enemy, but it's still early in the investigation. A lot more people to talk to now. Thanks for the tip on the band members."

I sighed. "I have one more tip for you and you may not like this one."

"Why wouldn't I like it?

"Well, it might muddy up your investigation a bit."

"How so?" Andre stretched the words out, his voice tight.

"When I talked to my mom yesterday, she said Marianne Hartman was really broken up about KJ. She's his godmother and when his mom died, KJ stayed with them for a while. So, do you kind of see where I'm going?"

"Joss, you're not trying to connect KJ's death with Vince's?"

I shrugged even though Andre couldn't see me. "I'm just saying that they knew each other. And both of them were tragically killed in a hit and run, one in a car and the other while walking and minding his business. Seems like someone has an M.O. using a car as a weapon."

"There's no hard evidence connecting the two cases."

"Okay. I was just putting it out there. Aren't we quite the pair, discussing murder and evidence before bedtime."

Andre chuckled. "Yes, we are. The woman of my dreams. No more crime solving for you tonight. I should be off early on Friday. Beckett and I agreed to take a break this weekend. Leads are slow, so I'll be there to help set up for Friday Night Jam."

"Great. I look forward to hanging out."

We said our goodnights.

I did stop thinking about the cold case as I drifted off to sleep. But only because I was thinking about what Andre had said.

Woman of my dreams.

That's what he said!

Wednesday, November 20 at 8:37 a.m.

Valerie must have been an early riser. From my notifications, her response came at five o'clock in the morning. That was way too early. I was comatose to the world at that hour. I read her message.

> **@fiercediva: Joss! I love your podcast! Great episode with Lily. Vince was the coolest brother. We can meet at my place after my 9:30 spin class. I'm done around 11 at the gym. Send me your number and I'll text you my address.**

I did as asked. With a few texts between us, we agreed to meet at one o'clock at her home.

By the time I'd showered and felt more awake, I noticed an email waiting for me from Carolyn Becker.

Subject: Re: Inquiry about Vince Hartman - Cold Justice Podcast

Dear Ms. Miller,

Thank you for reaching out. Vince was indeed a cherished member of our faculty, and his loss still weighs heavily on our school community.

I would be willing to meet with you Wednesday afternoon at the school. Would 4:30 work for you? My last student will have finished her piano lessons by then, and we'll have privacy to talk. Please park in the side lot and come to the front entrance. I will let my secretary know you're coming.

Sincerely,

Carolyn Becker, Director

Crescendo Music Academy

I sent a quick email to Carolyn letting her know I would see her at 4:30 p.m. this afternoon. Lily was really helping these episodes come together fast. Now I needed to figure out my questions. There would be no rest today on my day off.

I grabbed my backpack which had my MacBook and notebooks. At the top of the stairwell, something really good teased my nostrils. This time of year, Louise liked to bake, and I loved the coziness of the house when she ran the oven. I headed downstairs where Louise sat in the living room. On the television screen was one of those judge shows. I couldn't keep up with them, the only one I really recognized was Judge Judy and that wasn't her.

Louise waved at me. "You're going somewhere today, dear. I thought it was your day off."

"It is, but I have two interviews today for the podcast."

Louise clapped her hands together. "Oh, how nice. You sound like a reporter getting the story."

I laughed. "No, not a reporter. But this set of episodes has taken on a different tone than the last."

Louise rubbed Ginger's head, her forehead wrinkled in thought. "As long as you're being careful out there."

"I am. I'm going to grab some coffee and some breakfast. I need time to work on some questions."

"There are some fresh-baked cinnamon rolls on the counter. Be sure to get some."

She didn't need to ask me twice. Just what my sweet tooth needed. With a big cup of black coffee and two large cinnamon rolls, I settled at the kitchen table. It took me some time to scribble out questions for Valerie. Being Vince's sister, my questions needed to be even more sensitive. I was really curious about what she would say. I didn't have the best experience with her other brother last week. I was pretty sure he wouldn't want to talk to me, so at least one representative from the Hartman family was good enough for me.

The questions I had for Carolyn seemed more straightforward. My mom shared that Vince had trouble keeping a job, but it sounded like he'd finally found the right one sticking to what he loved – music. I would be curious to know what a co-worker could tell me compared to the conversation with Lily and the one coming up with Valerie. He must have meant a lot to the staff to keep his photo on their website after his death.

I peeked at the time and panicked. I had no idea how the hours swam by, but I needed to go. I called out to my grandmother and sprinted to my car. I grinned as the red paint glinted in the noonday sun. Though I had a little drama at Carlson Auto, it was well worth it. I'd only been in my new-to-me car for a week, but it felt like I'd had her for years. The GPS would certainly come in handy. That was a luxury I'd never had before. Since I barely had any time between the two interviews, I mapped out my route through traffic. Thankfully, Valerie's apartment wasn't too far from the school. Traffic would still be a pain though.

Valerie lived in an older home off Meeting Street. If I hadn't been paying attention to the one way streets, I would have been driving in circles. When I found her residence, I cringed at having to park my sparkly red baby in her narrow parking space.

Grateful for the backup camera, yet another luxury feature, I carefully maneuvered into her driveway.

I walked through a narrow alleyway and rounded the corner to a pale blue front door. After a moment, I heard footsteps coming down what sounded like stairs. Then the door swung open. Valerie Hartman stood before me dressed in a large sweatshirt and black leggings. Her hair stood up in a spiked hairdo.

"Joss Miller. It's so good to meet you in person." she said, stepping aside to let me in. "Come on in."

"Thank you. It's great to meet you as well." I followed Valerie up a deep wooden staircase. At the top of the staircase was a cozy living room filled with bursts of color from the throw pillows to the wall art. As I settled onto the cushioned sofa, I didn't know where to lay my eyes. The apartment reflected the fierce diva that was Valerie Hartman.

"Can I get you something to drink? I have water, tea or lemonade, the latter two are freshly made." Valerie gushed.

"Oh. I'll have some lemonade, thanks."

I grabbed my phone and notebook from my bag, feeling more at home than I expected. I glanced around the room. Valerie's artwork was eclectic, but the central theme depicted the beauty of African American culture and women with shapely bodies and big hair. Family photos arranged in a staggered gallery layout adorned one wall. Most of the pictures were of Vince with Valerie. He was much older than her. From the pictures, I guessed there was about a sixteen year difference between them, making Valerie a late baby. There was a photo of a teenage Vince holding a young Valerie on his hip. Then one of her in a cap and gown, her brother's arm was slung around her shoulders as if he was a proud father.

Another photo caught my attention, but Valerie returned with a tall glass of lemonade. I noticed she had a glass of water filled with what appeared to be cucumber slices.

I pointed to the glass. "I will have to take notes from you on keeping healthy."

"Oh, this," Valerie held up the glass. "I'm really big on hydration, especially after a workout. You have great skin and hair. I love your curls. I'm sure you are taking great care of yourself."

"I try." I gestured toward the wall. I see a lot of photos of Vince. He was clearly your favorite person."

Valerie glanced back, her eyes glassy for a few seconds. She blinked rapidly. "Yes, he was my favorite."

"Is that KJ? I mean Khalil Rogers."

Valerie raised an eyebrow at me. "Yes. You knew him?"

"I barely remember him, but he was a friend of my brother—Nate Miller."

Valerie's face brightened. "Oh, I think I remember a Nate. Did he play football?"

I nodded, "Yes, he did. Basketball, too. I'm sorry for your loss."

She perched on the armchair across from me. Her confidence seemed to wane. "Thanks, KJ wasn't really family. At least not mine. He was Marianne's godson and he stayed with them his senior year. He was ahead of me in class, but I liked him. Good guy. He loved Vince like a brother, more so than a father-figure. It would have hurt Vince's heart to know KJ died so young. He was an excellent musician; my brother taught him."

I wanted to ask if she'd thought about the similarities in their death but didn't want to get off track.

"So," she began, "you want to know about Vince?"

I nodded, "I sent you some questions. I try not to pull any surprises, but when we start talking, I may veer off a bit."

"Thanks, hon. I appreciate having the questions beforehand." She paused and opened her phone. "Do you always do these interviews in person?"

I offered an uneasy laugh since I would have to run to another interview after I left Valerie. "Yeah, but I'm still new at this."

Valerie leaned forward as if she had some secret that she wanted to share. "I used to host a fitness podcast. But I was able to interview guests from all over the country virtually. I kind of miss it. It's not hard to set up video conferencing if you want some tips."

"Thank you, I appreciate it. When I first started, a friend gave me access to a recording studio which worked well for my first season. I interviewed quite a few older people and they liked coming to a studio, found it very professional."

Valerie nodded, "That season was about your grandfather's murder."

"Yes, you listened to the episodes?"

Valerie took a sip from her glass. "I did. And I can tell from your thoughtful questions that you've done your research on me. I like your style. It's one of the reasons why I encouraged Lily to reach out to you."

That surprised me. I thought this was Lily's idea.

Valerie slid a bamboo coaster over from the center of the coffee table and sat down her glass. She narrowed her eyes, locking her gaze on me. "Before we start though, I'd like to make sure you understand a bit about me."

"Okay, sure."

"I'm the black sheep of the family." She laughed, but there was a bitterness to her tone. "Vince was the main person in the family who reached out to me." She looked away. "I miss him every single day. He had so much more life in him. I think for the first time in his life, he was just starting to be happy."

"With Lily?"

Valerie nodded. "He loved her. She was so different from Marianne, his first wife. But I'm sure you know. Some people felt he was going through a midlife crisis asking for a divorce. Maybe he was, but my brother smiled and laughed a whole lot more."

I inquired. "I guess the divorce threw Marianne off a bit."

Valerie sucked in a sharp breath. "Oh, it did. Marianne has to come out on top. Always. How dare my brother end their marriage? The one that she ruled. Full disclosure, I have no love for my former sister-in-law. Of course, I love Allison and I'm a great auntie. But Marianne is not the goody-two shoes she tries to portray. Under all that calm and collective interior is a very mean woman."

I tried to keep my face neutral, but I knew my eyes had to widen. My podcast wasn't about gossip or putting anyone down. Still I was curious. I sensed there was more brewing under the surface when I met Marianne on Sunday. I could tell she didn't like Lily but restrained from showing anything other than proper manners. "What is it about her?"

Valerie's expression tightened, she pursed her full lips. "Where do I even start? She's the reason for half the drama in Vince's life, even after the divorce."

I leaned forward, intrigued. "How so?"

"Marianne likes control," Valerie explained. "She ruled everything when she was married to Vince, and she never really stopped. Their daughter, the church, Vince – she always had to have her say."

I commented. "She runs her family business. Do you think that has to do with how she handles the people in her life?"

Valerie snapped her finger. "Look at you. So perceptive! That's exactly it. She's always managing, wanting everything perfect. Vince felt suffocated. And she has this way of wanting the spotlight on her. People tiptoe around her, catering to what she wants. When Vince started dating Lily, I believe Marianne started rumors about them even though they'd been divorced for months. She didn't want him to be happy around her."

I waited, not interrupting. This was a little too juicy to stop.

Valerie fumed. "I'm not saying my brother was a saint. He was a good looking guy and women loved him. But Lily got unfairly persecuted by people in the church." She stood, grabbed her glass. "Do you need a refill?"

I held up my hand. "I'm good."

Valerie walked into her kitchen and ran the water at the sink. I was glad we got some of this out of the way before the interview. I had great editing software, so I would have removed it anyway. Like my mother warned, the last thing I wanted to do was get on Marianne's bad side.

Valerie returned, her face apologetic. She crossed her arms. "I'm sorry. *That* woman still gets under my skin."

I sipped some of the lemonade. "Do you think Marianne could have had something to do with Vince's death?"

Valerie's eyes widened. "I... I don't know. I never thought... I means she's always so obsessed with maintaining her image, with keeping everything under her control. No, I can't see it. Marianne didn't mind making Lily and Vince uncomfortable, but she wouldn't hurt anyone. She's a self-righteous, God-fearing woman."

Curious, I asked, "How did the rest of your family react to Marianne?"

Valerie rolled her eyes. "They loved her. My mother would have preferred I acted more like Marianne. She was the perfect daughter-in-law. They still talked to each other even after the divorce. That irked Lily. I couldn't blame her."

"I actually met your brother Terrell at a car dealership recently," I said. "He seemed... upset when I mentioned Lily."

Valerie huffed. "Terrell. I'm not surprised."

"Really?"

Valerie sighed. "Vince was the oldest, the golden child. Terrell, being the middle child... Well, there's bound to be some resentment. Don't get me wrong, he admired his older brother. Always wanted Vince's approval, more so than our parents. But there were times Terrell seemed to hate him too."

"Hate. That's a strong emotion for a sibling to have for another sibling."

An uncomfortable laugh squeaked from Valerie, almost little girl like. "Well, there's the story of Cain and Abel. Siblings don't always get along."

I thought of my own brother who stayed away living his life. There was distance between us but never hate.

"What about you and Terrell? Were you two ever close?"

Valerie's mouth tightened. "Never. He was the baby of the family for almost ten years before I came along. Terrell made it his mission to torment his little sister. Even now, he still treats

me like I'm that annoying kid who ruined his perfect world."
She gave a slight shrug, but I could see the hurt in her eyes.

I wanted to ask if Valerie thought Terrell would harm his own
brother, but I sensed she was about to shut that conversation
down. I thought about the big man that loomed over me at the
car dealership, his unexpected anger.

Was he really upset about his brother's death or did he have
something to do with it?

At first, I wasn't sure about interviewing Vince's sister, but I
liked that she had a different perspective. Now I wondered if my
questions would do this episode justice. Valerie had expressed
her opinion about two people her brother had conflicts with,
but I could hear Andre's voice in my head.

Be careful!

"Are you ready to start recording?"

Valerie took a deep breath and nodded. "Let's do this."

I pressed the record button on my phone, and we began the
official interview.

COLD JUSTICE PODCAST, EPISODE #12
"A Christmas Eve Tragedy: Part 2"

Welcome back to the *Cold Justice* podcast. I'm your host, Joss Miller. In our ongoing investigation into the death of Vince Hartman, we've heard from his widow, Lily. Today, we're diving deeper into the Hartman family dynamics with a special guest: Valerie Hartman, Vince's younger sister.

Valerie offers us a unique perspective into her brother's life up until his tragic death.

Joss: Valerie, thank you for joining us today. Can you start by telling us about your relationship with your brother Vince?

Valerie: Of course, Joss. Vince and I were always close. Growing up, he was my protector, my confidant. Even as adults, we remained tight-knit. I saw sides of him that others didn't, including the struggles he faced in his personal life.

Joss: You mentioned struggles. Can you elaborate on that?

Valerie: Well, Vince always felt a lot of pressure. From our parents, from the church, and especially from his ex-wife, Marianne. He loved music and wanted to pursue it fully, but there were always expectations pulling him in different directions.

Joss: Sounds like he eventually found his sweet spot working at Crescendo Music Academy.

Valerie: Yes, the academy was his happy place. He lit up when he talked about his students and the choir.

Joss: I heard you set up Vince with his second wife. Can you tell us about Lily and Vince's relationship from your perspective?

Valerie: (laughs) I am known for being a very good matchmaker. Lily and I were friends first, actually. That's how she met Vince. He was older, but young at heart. You know black don't crack, so you couldn't really tell his age. (laughs) I was happy for them. Lily brought out a side of Vince I hadn't seen in years. He was lighter, more carefree.

Joss: How did others react to Vince and Lily's relationship?

Valerie: Unfair. Lily is the sweetest person. And she got all kinds of backlash. You would think people in the church would show love, but they were her worst critics. Vince and Lily didn't date until after the divorce was finalized, but I'm not going to get into all that on your podcast. I do want people to know that too many people were in my brother's business – as usual. Comes with the territory of being a renowned preacher's kid. I stopped going to Greater Zion myself. It became too much for my mental health.

Joss: I can understand that. Some people you least expect can be toxic. Speaking of mental health, Lily mentioned that you noticed something was off with Vince like she did. Can you tell us about that?

Valerie: Yes, that's true. A few days before... before it happened, I met Vince for coffee. He seemed distracted, almost jumpy. When I asked what was wrong, he brushed it off, said he was stressed about work. But that didn't make much sense, he worked at a music school. He was hiding something. I knew my brother. This was different.

Joss: Different how?

Valerie: He kept checking his phone, like he was expecting an important call or message. And at one point, he said something that stuck with me. He said, "Val, if anything ever happens to me, make sure Allison knows I love her. And you know how much I love you, kid." (Valerie chokes up) It was so out of the blue for him. I asked him what was going on, but he changed the subject.

Joss: Did you share these observations with anyone at the time?

Valerie: I told Lily, but it was too late then. And the cops never came to talk to me. They were too busy harassing Lily like she'd ran up on her husband and ran him off the road. There was no evidence at all.

Joss: Looking back now, do you think Vince might have been in some kind of trouble?

Valerie: [Long pause] I... I think he must have been. The Vince I saw that day was scared, Joss. He was trying to hide it, but I could tell. Something was terribly wrong, and now I can't help but wonder if it was connected to what happened to him.

Joss: Thank you, Valerie, for sharing these difficult memories with us. Is there anything else you think our listeners should know about Vince's last days?

Valerie: Someone knows what really happened that night. Vince was a good man. He loved his wife, his daughter, his family... he loved music, and in the end, I believe he was trying to find a way to be true to himself. Whatever happened to him, he didn't deserve it. I hope your podcast can help uncover the truth, Joss. My brother deserves that much.

Joss: And there you have it, listeners. A powerful and emotional account from Valerie Hartman, shedding new light on

Vince Hartman's state of mind in the days leading up to his death. We'll be digging deeper into Vince's final days with other guests in the coming days.

Remember, we're here to uncover the truth, wherever it may lead us. If you have any information related to this case, especially regarding Vince's activities in the week before his death, please reach out through our website or the CPD tip line.

Until next time, this is Joss Miller with the *Cold Justice* podcast.

Chapter 11
Troubled Melodies

Wednesday, November 20 at 4:21 p.m.

I arrived at the school earlier than I thought. Buzzed from the interview with Valerie, I wished I had time to process. I thought her idea about doing these interviews virtually would be something I considered for the future. I had a feeling I would be exhausted tomorrow from not fully enjoying my day off. I parked in the side parking lot as directed. There was only one other car in the parking lot, an older black Mercedes.

The sound of a piano melody greeted me as I stepped into the foyer of Crescendo Music Academy. The entrance was warmly lit with framed photos of smiling students and their instruments adorning the walls. Music floated down the hall and I could tell the fingers on the piano were still learning. Not that I was a musician, but even I could identify that the jarring key came from an amateur. I looked around and decided to head down the hallway, hoping it was Carolyn Becker with her student.

A petite woman with a gray afro was bent over a grand piano guiding a young girl's hands across the keys. The milk chocolate girl looked to be anywhere from ten to twelve years old. She wore cute ponytails on each side of her head. It was nice to see a young girl not appearing older than her age. I imagined her parents had certain expectations since she was taking piano lessons.

"That's it, Desiree," the woman encouraged. "Now, let's try that passage one more time."

I waited patiently, not wanting to interrupt the lesson. As the final notes faded, the woman straightened up and noticed me.

"Oh! You must be Joss," she said, her face breaking into a warm smile. "I'm Carolyn Becker. Just give me a moment to wrap up with Desiree here."

"No problem." I set my bag down and sank into a high back chair near the door. I watched as Carolyn gave Desiree some final instructions and a sticker for her progress chart. As the young girl packed up her music sheets, Carolyn turned to me. "Let me make sure Desiree's mom is outside and I will be right with you."

I nodded, taking out my notebook with the questions. I glanced around the cozy room. The small classroom also had comfortable chairs and a table. More photos of children with their instruments lined the wall. I noticed one photo in particular and stood from my chair.

It was Vince, laughing and smiling with a group of teens.

"He was such a treasure to this academy." A soft voice said behind me.

I turned to see Carolyn had reentered the room. I hadn't heard her, but the room was carpeted.

"Follow me to my office." Carolyn walked fast, chatting as we moved. "The sound is good in any of the rooms. I had that built into the walls years ago when the school was getting set up for students."

"I imagine that helps with keeping the music lessons contained to each classroom."

She laughed. "It would be headache-inducing if we didn't have some soundproof elements built in."

We entered a small office off the reception area. A window on the side of the large oak desk showed the busy traffic outside. Carolyn gestured for me to take a seat as she settled behind the desk cluttered with sheet music and more framed photos. These photos had children with similar features to Carolyn.

In one photo stood a tall man, who I assumed was Carolyn's husband.

Carolyn took a breath as if preparing herself for the conversation.

"I really appreciate you talking to me today. I was visiting with Valerie, Vince's sister earlier this afternoon."

Carolyn smiled. "That's lovely. Valerie was Vince's pride and joy. He always talked about what a lovely voice she had and how he wished he could get her to come back to church and sing for him."

"It sounded like they were very close. I've heard good things about Vince's time here too."

Carolyn's voice shook a bit. "Vince was one of our most popular instructors. The students adored him. He had this way of bringing out the best in everyone he taught. That's what made him a popular choir director too."

I nodded, pulling out my phone and sitting it on the edge of her desk. "Would you mind if I record our conversation for the podcast?"

"Not at all, dear, but—" She held her hand up to stop me from pressing record. "Can we talk a bit off the record?"

My smile wavered. "Sure."

She folded her hands in front of her on the desk. "I founded this school over ten years ago. I value my reputation and I want to protect the school. Parents and guardians entrust me with their children, to teach them how to play music and hone their voices. You're probably wondering where I'm going with this."

I was but wasn't going to ask. "I like for my guests to be comfortable with the conversation. Did you get a chance to view the questions I sent earlier?"

She smiled. "Yes, the questions are fine. I guess what I'm trying to get at is I don't want any trouble. I talked to Lily's mother. That's how I know Lily. Evelyn teaches here part-time. Lily was one of my first students when I opened. She has a beautiful voice that the world doesn't hear much of now. I want to help her find out what happened to Vince, but I don't want the extra talk that comes from social media to reflect back on the school or me. Does that make sense?"

"Absolutely. You know when I started this podcast it really was about putting a light on the victim. That's what I want to do, but I realized from my last podcast series, the one I did on Rebecca Montgomery, that sometimes the truth comes out and the perpetrator can be caught."

Carolyn smiled. "I knew Rebecca. It's sad what happened to her. I hope that evil man is sent away for the rest of his life."

Me too. Not many people in the public knew about Caleb coming after me. I don't know how it was kept as quiet as it was, but I was grateful only those closest to me knew.

I studied the woman. Carolyn's age was hard to guess. I assumed she was in her late forties or early fifties based on her illustrious bio. She'd had a career before she established this school over ten years ago. But I had a feeling the lines and strain around her eyes were a result of something else.

"Did you notice something about Vince before his death?"

Carolyn stared at me, but she didn't seem to be looking at me. She seemed to be in some struggle within her mind about what to say. Maybe she was wanting to back out of the interview and trying to find a polite way to do so. When she finally focused on my face, she said.

"Yes, I think Vince was in serious trouble."

Wednesday, November 20 at 4:49 p.m.

My body tingled and the hair stood up on my arm from Carolyn's statement. I could tell she was afraid. Her information could be what was needed for the investigation.

"Did the police talk to you?"

Carolyn shook her head. "They came to visit the classroom where Vince taught. There was nothing there for them to find. They took his laptop, but they didn't question me much. To be honest, it's been almost a year. I've had a lot of time to think and maybe I've been overthinking. Sometimes we see things differently later on, but that doesn't make it true."

"What did you see?"

Carolyn gulped. "It wasn't so much what I saw, but how Vince changed. He was the kind of man who was always smiling, joking, a very charming man. He was really frustrated and curt, even with the students, that last week before his death. When I first heard about his accident, I thought maybe he'd had a heart attack behind the wheel."

That was interesting. "Was he under some stress here at the school?"

"No. Well, we were preparing for the annual Christmas pageant. But he was passionate about it and the children did well. It was something else. I'm not a gossip, but I did ask Evelyn if everything was going well at home with Vince and Lily. They were still newlyweds, and there could be issues."

"What did Lily's mom say?"

"She said the trouble was more with Vince's family. They weren't happy with him marrying Lily. Also, well, he and his brother had an argument." Carolyn pointed, "Right out there in the parking lot."

"Vince argued with Terrell?"

Carolyn nodded. "Terrell had borrowed his brother's car. I'm not sure if he damaged it or something, but Vince was livid. He never seemed to recover his good attitude after that argument. I wondered if it was something else going on between the two brothers."

Valerie admitted earlier that Terrell had a love-hate relationship with his older brother.

"But you didn't share this with the police?" I inquired.

Carolyn shook her head. "I didn't think about it then. But I knew that incident put Vince on edge. He stayed that way the last few days he was here. I asked him about it, but he stated he was fine. And that everything would be fine after the holidays. But…" Her voice caught. "He didn't make it to Christmas."

Carolyn grabbed a tissue.

"I'm sorry," I pointed to my phone. "If this is too upsetting, I can come back. Or, if you don't want to do this anymore, I understand."

"No, I want to talk about Vince. I want to tell the world what a good man he was and what he did for the students here. I felt the need to tell you these things. Talking out loud helped me, but I do want to be cautious about what is published."

I nodded. "You don't have to say any names. I did that with my first podcast. Even though it was pretty well-known about the people involved in my grandfather's death, I didn't name them. I can press record when you're ready."

Carolyn wiped her moist eyes with the tissue. "Okay." She offered me a brief nod, and I pressed the record button.

I couldn't help but think that Carolyn may have dropped more clues than expected. It was often the ones closest to you who could do the most harm.

COLD JUSTICE PODCAST, EPISODE #13
"A Christmas Eve Tragedy: Part 3"

Joss: Welcome back to the *Cold Justice* podcast. I'm your host Joss Miller. In our ongoing investigation into the death of Vince Hartman, we've heard from his widow, Lily, and his sister, Valerie. Today, we're exploring another facet of Vince's life — his passion for music and teaching.

Our guest is Carolyn Becker, owner of Crescendo Music Academy where Vince taught up until his untimely passing. Mrs. Becker will share about Vince's professional life and his impact on his students.

As always, we encourage our listeners to approach all information with an open and critical mind as we continue to piece together the events surrounding Vince's death.

And now, let's hear from Carolyn Becker.

Joss: Mrs. Becker, thank you for speaking with us today. Can you start by telling us about the Crescendo Music Academy and what you offer students.

Carolyn: Thank you for having me, Joss. Crescendo Music Academy began as a dream of mine over ten years ago. After years of performing across Europe, I felt called to return home to Charleston and create something meaningful here. We started small, with me teaching piano lessons.

Over the years, we've grown into a full music education center. We offer private lessons in piano, strings, and voice, as well as group classes in music theory.

Joss: Tell us more about Vince's role at Crescendo Music Academy?

Carolyn: Of course. Vince was one of our most beloved instructors. He had a special way with the students. They absolutely adored him. Vince helped build our choral program. He had this remarkable ability to bring out the best in every voice, even the most timid children.

Joss: How long had Vince been teaching at the academy?

Carolyn: Oh, let's see... It must have been about five years. He started part-time, you know, a few hours a week. But as his popularity grew, so did his hours. By the end, he was here almost every day.

Joss: Did you notice any changes in Vince's behavior or mood in the weeks leading up to his death?

Carolyn: [Pauses] He did seem a bit distracted in his last week. But I assumed it was stress from balancing his work here with his duties at the church. We had the annual Christmas pageant, but practice was going well. The pageant occurred a few days before Christmas. He also did the annual program at Greater Zion. I honestly don't know how he did both.

Joss: What were some clues to his distraction?

Carolyn: Well, he missed a couple of staff meetings, which wasn't like him at all. And once or twice, I caught him on his phone during breaks between lessons, looking quite serious. But whenever I asked if everything was alright, he'd smile and say it was nothing to worry about.

Joss: Did Vince ever mention any conflicts or problems he was having, either at work or in his personal life?

Carolyn: [Hesitates] I... I'm not one to gossip, you understand. But there was one day, about a week before the accident, when I overheard him arguing with someone outside. I couldn't make out what was being said, but... I will say it was a family member. Probably not a big deal. When Vince saw me afterward, he looked embarrassed and said it was a misunderstanding.

Joss: Did you believe his explanation?

Carolyn: At the time, yes. Vince was always so honest and straightforward. But now, looking back... I'm not sure. I mean it was family and it's understandable he wanted to be quiet about it.

Joss: Mrs. Becker, is there anything else you think our listeners should know about Vince?

Carolyn: Just that he was a truly special person. He touched so many lives here at the academy. The students, the parents, all of us on staff, we all miss him terribly.

Many people don't know this, but Vince also had a lot of influence and respect within the gospel industry. I hope your podcast can help uncover the truth. He deserves that much.

Joss: Thank you, Mrs. Becker, for sharing your memories and insights with us.

And there you have it, listeners. Mrs. Becker established Vince as a dedicated teacher and musician.

Remember, if you have any information, please reach out or call the CPD tip line. Any detail could be the key to unlocking this mystery.

Until next time, this is Joss Miller for the *Cold Justice* podcast.

Chapter 12
Friday Night Jam

Friday, November 22 at 8:08 p.m.

I had quite the full week starting with the grand jury and then kicking off a new case with Lily's interview. This was a first for me, wrapping up two more episodes in the same week. I could barely keep up. The combination of Lily and Valerie's interviews had brought more traffic than I'd seen with the first two cases combined. I decided to wait to release the interview with Carolyn on Monday.

One constant with Friday Night Jams was our significant others made it a point to provide manpower for their women. Joe and Andre showed up a little before six o'clock to set up the new chairs that came with the center. It was good to hang out with my boyfriend for a change, even if we were both hustling to get set up for the night's activities.

I knew he had to be tired, but he'd gotten a haircut and managed to shave. Wearing an outfit that was nothing like his usual suit and tie detective's uniform, Andre looked pretty relaxed in jeans and a short-sleeve polo shirt emblazoned with Sugar Creek Café Staff. He and Joe were cutting up as they carried chairs.

Courtesy of our sponsors, the local tech company, Synaptic, we had burgundy chairs with nice cushions for sitting. They'd even donated flat screens that would be awesome to use during presentations. The empty center was looking like we'd envisioned, filled with enough chairs to seat seventy-five people and plenty of space for a dancefloor off to the side. It was still amazing to think that this was once a craft store.

DJ Nyla B came in shortly after we had the chairs in place to set up her equipment. As a female DJ, she stayed booked. But as a friend of mine, she kept Friday Night Jams on her schedule. She kept the jam going while the live band took a break.

Fay's sisters came out to volunteer and were admitting guests as they showed up. Most people wandered around the center checking out the small collection of Rebecca Montgomery's artwork and that of a few other local artists on display.

With the new center, we were able to keep the café open for food and drink. Extra hands were needed tonight, which meant every Sugar Creek Café employee was on hand except Briana. As lead singer for Indigo Soul, she was all about the performance tonight. I hadn't heard her sing in quite some time and couldn't wait.

The center filled up nicely with all age groups, young and old. I was enjoying the vibe when I felt familiar arms around me. At first, I was a little embarrassed by the public affection, but then I realized how much I missed Andre and leaned into him.

He said in my ear. "The center turned out really nice. I guess I can't hate on Ethan Turner too much since he made all this possible." The owner of Synaptic had been Rebecca Montgomery's boyfriend, and this center was his way of honoring her as well as giving back to the community. The tech mogul wasn't a favorite on Andre's list.

"This was a great investment." I turned to look up at him, forgetting that there were people around us. "I've missed you."

He stared into my eyes. "Likewise. Hopefully we're not too tired to get some dancing in before the night is over."

"Oh, I will find the energy." I teased. I knew Fay wouldn't mind if we took a break. We were going to be here late doing cleanup. It was going to be a long, but fun, night.

"Well, well. You two are adorable together!"

I turned to see Sophia Carlson beaming at us, her perfectly styled bob swinging. I hadn't even noticed her approach.

"Hey, Sophia. Good to see you again."

Sophia's eyes darted between us with undisguised interest. "Is this your husband, Joss?"

"Not yet," Andre answered smoothly before I could respond, giving my hand a gentle squeeze.

I giggled, though I wasn't sure if I should have been annoyed by her assumption. At my age, twenty-eight, and especially with how affectionate Andre and I were, church folks tended to jump to conclusions.

"Oh, how sweet," Sophia beamed. "Sounds like you have yourself a keeper. I do a little wedding planning on the side if you need my services."

Whoa, woman, slow down.

I glanced at Andre, whose eyes widened as well.

Grant Carlson appeared, saving us from anymore awkwardness. He slid his arm around Sophia's waist. Together, they looked like they'd stepped out of a magazine. They really were a striking couple.

"I hope you're still enjoying the car?" Grant asked, flashing his salesman smile.

"I am, thank you for your help last week."

Grant cocked his finger in the air. "Remember to tell all your friends about Carlson Auto. Best deals in Charleston." He peered down at his wife. "Shall we find some seats?"

Sophia beamed at her husband. Before they moved on, she stated, "You two be good."

Andre chuckled. "Quite the salesman, that one."

I was too busy wanting to tell Sophia Carlson to mind her business. She didn't know me. We'd only met this past Sunday.

I frowned as I watched the couple mingle with the crowd. They were quite charming and seemed to know a lot of people. Lily said they were one of Greater Zion's royal families. Between the megachurch and selling cars, I supposed knowing a lot of people wasn't surprising. I wondered what happened to Terrell after that scene at the dealership last week. The memory of Vince Hartman's brother growing angry still bothered me, especially after my conversations with Valerie and Carolyn.

Just how volatile was the relationship between the two brothers? I found it odd that Valerie mentioned Cain and Abel.

The older brother didn't survive that sibling rivalry.

I glanced over at the door. Lily was there greeting Fay. Indigo Soul had arrived thirty minutes ago. All the band members, including Jake, were in one of the classrooms near the stage. We turned it into a last minute dressing room. I thought about how the two exes were in an intense conversation outside the café earlier this week, they were bound to run into each other tonight. And a lot more people would witness them together.

But was that really a bad thing? Lily had become a widow tragically. She had to move on with her life. It was pretty obvious to me, and probably others, that Jake never lost his feelings for her.

Did Lily really love Vince the way she loved Jake? I wished we had talked more about that during my interview with her, but it wasn't relevant.

Andre turned to look at who caught my attention. "There is your star interviewee. What are you thinking about?"

I grinned. This man knew me too well. "I'm probably thinking too much. I'm keeping an open mind like you asked me to."

Andre crossed his arms. "You have to have one when you're an investigator. I wish we could solve every homicide that came our way and that none of them would grow cold. But leads get missed or end up going nowhere."

"Well, if cases never went cold, I wouldn't have a podcast, sweetie. *Cold Justice* podcast, duh!"

Andre shook his head and chuckled. "Your humor is turning as bad as a cop's. I'm starting to wonder if I'm really a good influence."

I grabbed his arm. "You are the best."

At that moment, Indigo Soul stepped out behind their instruments. Briana wore a sexy red dress and headed to the mic. The band started playing and Briana delivered hot vocals to a Chaka Khan oldie, "Tell Me Something Good." The crowd gathered, but there was still a lot more room in the center than there had been inside the café.

"Hey." Andre touched my chin, bringing my focus back to him. "You promised me a dance, remember?"

"I'm ready."

Andre led me over to the floor and surprisingly, we found the energy to dance. It wasn't hard. Indigo Soul played excellent covers of every song. We danced through two funky songs until Indigo Soul decided to take a break.

Thirsty and ready to sit down, we crossed over into the café. Andre grabbed us a booth while I went behind the counter to fix us both iced coffees. Temperatures had dropped down to the late forties, but we could handle the cold drinks. I scooted in across from Andre, who, by habit, liked to sit with his eyes on doorways. Even though he was off, the cop part of him switched on as he surveyed people in line and sitting around the café.

I noticed a couple in the back.

"What's up?" Andre asked, starting to turn.

"Don't turn around." I whispered.

Andre rolled his eyes. "Yes, ma'am."

I took a sip of my iced coffee. "I see Lily and Jake found each other." I glanced around. No one was near us. "Hypothetically, a wife could benefit from a husband's accident, insurance-wise, right?"

Andre raised an eyebrow. "Hypothetically, yes." He leaned forward. "Who benefits are one of the things investigators look at when checking out spouses. What are you thinking?"

I shrugged. "It's interesting after being out of sight for a year being the grieving widow, now she's showing interest in the man that she'd been with before she got married."

Andre took a sip and looked out the window. He turned back to me. "It's suspicious. But both of them were checked out. Solid tight alibis."

I lifted my hands in mock surrender. "I'm just throwing out theories. I've talked to two other women who were close to Vince and they both had interesting things to say."

Andre asked, "I heard what his sister Valerie had to say in the episode. Something or someone, rather, had Vince uptight. The question is who would that have been?"

I agreed. "I'll send you Carolyn's interview so you can listen to it before I publish it on Monday. She had more concrete things to say. She wasn't bashing anyone but as a concerned colleague, she did mention a conflict with a family member."

Andre froze and looked at me. "She didn't name the family member in the podcast?"

"No, of course not. We talked before the recording so I can tell *you* who she was referring to." I looked around again and then back at Andre before whispering, "Terrell."

Andre cocked an eyebrow. "He definitely has a temper."

"And works at a car dealership with access to cars. I wonder why no one at CPD talked to Mrs. Becker."

"I don't know. You know us cops are mainly homed in on getting the suspect. In this case, we start with the spouse." Andre tilted his head. "I'm not making excuses. Too many cases, too little time."

"I know, I know. Did you want anything else?" I gave him a toothy grin. "Being an employee, I can skip the line."

Andre shook his head. "I'm good sitting here."

I hopped up. This was nice, even though we were at the place where I worked, it was almost like being on a date. It had been awhile.

Behind us the door between the café and the center opened with high-pitched laughter. I turned my head to catch a glimpse at the definitely female voices and froze.

"Oh no." I muttered.

This could be trouble.

Friday, November 22 at 8:34 p.m.

Allison Hartman entered the café with two girls around her age. As they approached the line, the teen I'd seen at church was almost unrecognizable. She waved her hands wildly while chatting with her friends. When I was sitting down at Greater Zion, I didn't realize how tall she was. She stood a few inches over the other girls. Upon closer examination, she wore a full make-up face with false eyelashes so thick I was surprised the girl could see.

She was a beautiful girl, reminding me of her aunt Valerie, except with longer hair and lots of baby hair around her temples. I wondered if Allison came with her aunt. Teens were allowed to come to Friday Night Jam since we kept it family friendly. We had an age limit of thirteen years and up, but teens were encouraged to have an adult with them. I didn't see any adults and doubted Marianne would approve of her daughter's behavior. Or appearance. The blouse she wore dipped lower in the cleavage region than even I was comfortable wearing, and I didn't mind taking chances on outfits.

Andre followed my gaze. "Do you know those girls?"

"The one in the middle is Vince's daughter."

I glanced around in the back corner and saw that Lily had also noticed Allison. She stood and began walking over to the teen, a concerned look on her face.

My stomach knotted as Jake followed Lily. I whispered to Andre. "This may not be good."

I hated being right but cringed when I saw Allison's eyes lock on Lily. The teenager stopped talking mid-sentence, her face transformed into rage in an instant. "Are you kidding me?" she practically shrieked.

One of her friends, the shortest one with glasses, grabbed her arms. "Allie, don't—"

Allison shook off her friend's hand. "Really? You couldn't even wait a year? My dad's not even cold in his grave and you're already back with him?"

The café fell silent. I glanced at Andre, who'd had that watchful look that cops get during trouble. He may have been in civilian clothes, but he looked ready to spring into action.

It concerned me, how hostile Allison was toward Lily. The teenager looked ready to fight the older woman. I peered closer at her and wondered if she may have been drinking or on something.

Jake moved forward in a protective stance in front of Lily. "We're just talking. You don't need to make a scene."

Lily put a hand on his arm, pulling him back. She took a step closer to the teen. "Allison, sweetheart—"

"Don't you 'sweetheart' me!" Allison's voice cracked as she backed up. She waved her hands in front of her, pointing in their direction. "You're disgusting! Both of you!"

Her friends tried again to pull her back. "Come on, Allie, let's go back—"

But Allison had grown unhinged. Tears formed in her eyes. "No! Everyone needs to see what kind of person she really is!"

This was certainly not normal behavior. I wanted to do something, but I wasn't sure what I thought I could do. Before I could step closer, Fay appeared from the back, her former teacher's voice firm, but gentle. "Allison, that's enough. I've already called your mother. You all shouldn't be here without a chaperone."

The fight drained from Allison's face, replaced by fear. "You... you called my mom?"

"Yes, and she's on her way." Fay's tone softened. "Why don't you and your friends take a seat at a booth? You can wait for her there."

Allison's shoulders slumped. "I'm sorry, Ms. Fay. I didn't mean to..." She glanced around the silent café, her eyes wide with embarrassment. "I'm sorry," she repeated, her voice barely above a whisper. She let her friends guide her toward a booth next to where Andre and I sat.

Andre grabbed my hand and squeezed. "That poor kid. Fay did the right thing."

I nodded, but I still felt compelled to do something. I understood grief, missing your dad. I turned as the girls settled into the booth. "Would any of you like anything while you wait? My treat. I work here."

Allison seemed to ball up into herself not looking at me. She stared down at the table. The smaller girl with glasses smiled. "We were coming for the hot chocolate."

I grinned back. "That sounds good. Let me get those for you."

I glanced at Andre, who gave me a nod as he settled back down in the booth. When I turned around I locked eyes with Lily. "She will be fine. I'm going to grab some hot chocolate for them."

Lily looked back behind me. "She's grieving. I know Fay thought she was helping by calling Marianne, but it might have been better to call Valerie instead."

I looked back. Allison appeared like a completely different person. I recognized this girl, the one who shrunk inside herself when her mother was around. "Maybe we can still call Valerie too."

Lily blew out a breath. "And have her run into Marianne? That would be a far worse outcome to have."

Jake grabbed Lily's elbow. "Why don't we go back into the center? It's about time for the band to get back onstage for our next set. I wish you were still singing with us."

Lily shook her head. "That's behind me for now. Besides, Briana really knows how to work the crowd. I like her. Her voice is much stronger than mine."

I liked that Lily showed respect to Briana. I went behind the counter and started to prep the hot chocolate. Fay came up beside me. "How is Allison doing?"

I shrugged. "She's definitely quieter. Do you think Marianne will cause a scene?"

Fay shook her head. "No. She will get the girls home."

I bent down in the fridge and pulled out some whip cream. "Allison is wearing make-up and looks older. If Marianne is like my mom, she will not like that."

Fay sighed, "Knowing Marianne, she will have plenty to say. Hey, don't worry about the hot chocolate. I appreciate you taking care of them."

I grinned. "Chocolate chip cookies go well with this too."

She rolled her eyes. "Whatever." Fay could be tough, but she was a softie too. I placed three cookies and three hot chocolates on a tray. The perfect comfort food for a pity party.

As I walked back over, I noticed Andre was on his phone. I sat the tray down and Allison's friends started oohing and aahing over the cookies. Allison finally looked up due to the commotion her friends made. She glanced at the tray and then at me. I smiled at her.

"This is the podcaster." Allison gestured toward me. Both girls looked up at me, admiration on their faces.

"That must be so cool."

"I would love to do that."

Both girls talked at once.

I laughed. "It's a pretty exciting hobby to have." I held my hand up to my ear. "Allison, did you hear the podcast this morning with your aunt?"

She nodded, her face a bit more lively now. "Yeah. You could talk to me too. I'm almost eighteen." She nudged the friend next to her. "Tell her."

Her other friend had braces. When she grinned, the light bounced off the silver. "Her birthday is the day after Christmas."

"Oh, you must get double gifts." I said.

Allison crinkled her face. "Yeah, it's not all that fun."

I bet so. Especially with the anniversary of her dad's death on Christmas Eve. Every day is painful after the loss of a loved one, but holidays and birthdays were more in your face, all those past memories were all you had.

Something caught my attention outside the window. I wasn't sure when she drove up or where she parked, but Marianne Hartman walked past the café window.

She did not look happy.

Friday, November 22 at 8:55 p.m.

Allison must have caught sight of her mother too. She hunched her shoulders as if preparing to get smacked. Even her two friends looked scared. One sipped their hot chocolate and the other chewed thoughtfully on a cookie. Allison hadn't touched either. Instead, she sat with her arms folded across her chest.

Thankfully, Indigo Soul had started up a new set, and the music blasting from the center drew people out of the café and back over to enjoy the live music. Fay stood behind the counter with one of the baristas. I walked back to the booth and climbed in next to Andre this time. I didn't really want to face Marianne, but I was curious how she handled her daughter.

Marianne rushed in, looking worn and exhausted. There were dark circles etched under her eyes. That's when I remembered that Marianne was grieving her godson. KJ. I wondered if being a funeral director made it even harder to do her job. I would have gladly passed the task to someone else.

She marched up to the counter. "I am so sorry about this, Fay," Marianne said. "Where is she?"

Fay pointed to the booth.

Marianne whipped around, her face blank where I expected to see rage. I imagined Marianne had to keep her emotions in check as a part of her job as a funeral director. The only sign of any anger was her stilted walk over to the booth where the girls sat. "Tabitha and Sandra, I will drop you off at home. Can you give me and Allison a minute? You can wait over there by the door."

Both friends quickly scooted out of the booth, taking their hot chocolate cups.

Allison's eyes flashed defiantly. "I know I was wrong, but I was shocked seeing Lily with her ex. That's not fair."

Marianne heaved a sigh. She must have noticed that Andre and I were in the booth. She looked over at us. Emotion flashed in her eyes, and she pointed at me. "You weren't trying to talk to my daughter."

I held up my hands in surrender. "No, of course not."

Allison shoved out of the booth. "Mom, stop. She isn't going to let me be on the podcast. But you can."

"What?" Marianne looked at her daughter incredulously.

Somehow finding a way to get the focus off her behavior, Allison gushed. "Aunt Val talked about Dad. That episode went out this morning."

Marianne sighed. "Did she now? Well, I'm sure she had much to say."

Since we were talking about my podcast, I added, "I also talked to Carolyn Becker. Vince had a good thing going at Crescendo Music Academy."

Marianne's eyes widened. "Carolyn talked to you too? What does all this talking do?" She placed her hands on her hips, her lip turned up in disgust. "It doesn't bring Vince back."

There was silence after Marianne's statement as she glared at me. Next to me, Andre had been quiet, but I felt him tense.

Allison broke the silence. "I know you don't care about my dad, but some of us want to know what happened to him." The teen's voice broke as tears ran down her face. "People stopped talking about him as if he never existed."

"Allie..." Marianne reached for her daughter, but Allison scrambled away, heading to where her friends stood watching. Both girls huddled around Allison as if to protect her.

Marianne lifted her eyes up to the ceiling. "Lord, what am I going to do?"

The answer must have come to her quickly. She took a deep breath and eyed me. "I will talk to you on your podcast. I don't know what I can say. But I guess by now people want to know what I have to say about Vince."

Kind of shocked at the turn around, I said. "I can reach out to you for a day and time."

"Thanksgiving is coming up next week. I'd like to do it before then. A lot of family will be in, especially those mourning KJ." She started to walk away and then turned around. "I know you concentrate on cold cases, but my godson hasn't been dead but a few days. People should be talking about why that young man's life was cut so short. He didn't deserve to die like that."

Did she think Vince deserved how he died?

Andre and I watched her walk away. I squeezed his hand. Marianne couldn't have known Andre was a detective on the case.

He looked at me. "I'm doing my best to make sure the trail doesn't grow cold for KJ like it did for Vince."

"You still don't think there's a connection? I mean is it really a coincidence that they died from hit and runs?"

Andre put his arm around me. "I'm looking into it. You watch your step. There's a lot of emotions flying around that family."

I wondered if someone in that family let their emotions go too far.

Chapter 13
Setting the Record Straight

Monday, November 25 at 7:55 p.m.

The episode with Carolyn Becker went surprisingly well. In fact, it went a bit viral. Being well-known in the music industry, Carolyn's episode attracted celebrities who left comments. I also hadn't realized Vince's reach was so well known beyond Greater Zion's walls and within the national gospel community. He was indeed a talented man.

But he wasn't loved by everyone.

Especially the person who ran him off the road.

His first wife had long since stopped being a fan, but she'd been willing to talk to me this evening. I decided to take Valerie's advice and do my first virtual interview. I had encountered Marianne in person and had heard much about her. A screen in between us would suit me fine.

I settled into my chair, adjusting my headphones and the new microphone I bought from Best Buy. When I logged into Zoom, no one was there yet. But I'd jumped on a few minutes early. Leesa let me practice with her last night, and then I tried it again with Andre. All I needed was good quality audio for the podcast.

While I fiddled with the settings, a black screen popped up. I straightened. A few seconds later, Marianne Hartman sat with a composed expression. But we weren't alone. Another screen popped up.

I don't know how she convinced her mother, but Allison appeared in what looked like her bedroom behind her. Her mother sat in an office.

"Oh, well, it's good to have you both on the podcast." I smiled, acting like I knew what was going on. I'd only prepared questions for Marianne.

What could Allison bring to the table? I had some questions that I wanted to ask her mother before we got started.

Marianne nodded, her lips pressed into a thin line. "We appreciate the opportunity, Ms. Miller. Allison is here because this was her idea. I want her to feel like she has her say, but I don't expect her to be recorded."

"Mom—" Allison started.

"Okay, that's fine. This is the first time I'm using Zoom. I normally like to talk to get us comfortable with the conversation." I took a deep breath and leaned forward. "I want to set some ground rules. This interview is about remembering Vince and sharing any concerns you have. I'm not here to create conflict or sensationalize anything. My goal is to gather information that might help us understand what happened. Are you both comfortable with that?"

Marianne's posture relaxed slightly. "That's fine with us. I listened to the interview with Carolyn. Saw what some people mentioned about him. I know he would appreciate that his legacy and love for gospel music continues to be respected."

Allison's eyes darted nervously into the camera.

I could sense there was something she wanted to say. Since her mother didn't want her recorded, I decided to do an unofficial interview. "Allison, for starters, do you want to talk about your father? I lost my dad a few days before I turned twenty, so I know a little about what you're going through."

Allison looked at me through the screen. "Was he in an accident?"

I sighed. I'd opened this door, but it was never easy for me. "No, he got sick. Colon cancer. He found out my senior year of high school, but only he and my mom knew. Eventually, he had to tell me and my brother. He was getting so skinny." Tears sprang to my eyes. "I did get a chance to say goodbye. It was the hardest goodbye I've ever had to do."

Allison's eyes glistened. "I didn't get a chance to say goodbye. I was looking forward to him coming to Grandma's house. Dad was a lot of fun, always singing. We were really close."

I smiled. "I was a daddy's girl too."

Allison sniffled. "I miss him. He always made time to listen to me, even after he married Lily. It's... it's been really hard without him."

I glanced over at Marianne. She looked heartbroken as if she hadn't known how her daughter felt. "So, I've talked to Lily, Valerie and Carolyn. All of them noticed a similar pattern. Did you notice if anything was different about your dad? I know you really wanted to talk."

Marianne looked like she wanted to object.

I reminded her. "I'm not recording. We're just talking. It's good to talk."

Allison looked down like she had to think about it. She lifted her head, her eyes troubled. "He seemed stressed. More than usual, I mean. That time of year, he always spent a lot of time at the school and church. He worked on Christmas programs at both. He liked everything to be perfect."

Marianne muttered. "Yes, he did."

Allison continued, "I heard him arguing on the phone a few days before. Do you think my dad was in some kind of trouble?"

I glanced at Marianne since I wasn't sure how to answer that.

Marianne appeared uncomfortable with the question as well. I wondered if she knew something but didn't want to reveal it in front of her daughter.

Finally, I said. "My prayer is that with the podcast, the police will look into what happened again with new eyes."

Allison nodded. "I used to think it was Lily's fault."

Marianne asked. "Why did you think that?"

Allison blew out a breath. "I heard they argued so loud the neighbors heard them. If they hadn't argued, maybe he wouldn't have been upset driving."

Marianne held her head down. "I know it's easier to want to blame someone, but we need the right person to pay."

"Thanks for letting me talk. I'm going to get off here. I have homework to finish."

"Bye, Allison. I appreciate you sharing."

I waited until she left the meeting and then looked at Marianne.

"So, I sent you some questions. Did you get a chance to look over them?"

She looked at me. "Yes, I did. I will be as candid as I can. I fell out of love with Vince a long time ago, as he did with me. The divorce wasn't a surprise, but I never expected him to file. We were the it couple in the church. A lot of people looked up to us like they did our parents. I won't disrespect my daughter's father, but I do think the world needs to know that trouble stirred around Vince whether he wanted it to or not."

"Okay, let's do this," I said more to myself than to Marianne. I pressed record and hoped this episode wouldn't blow up in my face.

COLD JUSTICE PODCAST, EPISODE #14
"A Christmas Eve Tragedy: Part 4"

Joss: Welcome back to the *Cold Justice* podcast. I'm your host, Joss Miller. Over the past week, we've been discussing the death of Vince Hartman, the beloved choir director of Greater Zion Church. We've heard from his widow, Lily Hartman, about their last argument on that fateful night. His younger sister, Valerie Hartman, revealed concerns about her brother's state of mind in his final weeks. His boss, singing legend Carolyn Becker, shared some disturbing patterns as well.

Today, we're speaking with someone who knew a different side of Vince— Marianne Hartman, his first wife. This interview may challenge some of what we think we know about Vince Hartman. Thank you for joining us, Marianne.

Marianne: Thank you for having me, Ms. Miller. I want to be clear that I'm here to tell the truth, not to destroy Vince's memory.

Joss: I understand. Can you tell us about Vince, from your perspective?

Marianne: (long pause) Vince was... complicated. He could charm anyone with that smile and that voice of his. I'd known him a long time, ever since we were in elementary school. His dad was a bishop, and my dad was a bishop. The Hartmans and the Danvers were friends. I went to my high school prom with Vince. From there, I think our families naturally thought we were a good fit.

Joss: Did you think you were a good fit?

Marianne: (laughs) Yes, for a long while, I did. The early years of marriage are always different. Vince could make you feel like you were the only person in the room. Later, I started to notice he made everyone feel that way. It wasn't just with women, though there was plenty of that. It was with anyone. It was his personality.

Joss: I looked into some of the things Vince did outside of the choir. He really found his stride as an instructor at the Crescendo Music Academy. But that took a while.

Marianne: (sighs) Yes. That's where our marriage started to break down. Vince wanted to do music all the time. But music didn't pay the bills. I found myself eventually taking over the family business so bills got paid, but I didn't always get support from Vince. The breaking point was when his brother got involved some get-rich-quick scheme. Vince could never say no to family. He'd sunk money into this hair-brained idea his brother cooked up. It was hard to recover from that and I was livid.

Joss: Were the financial issues the only issues that caused problems in your marriage?

Marianne: [sharp laugh] Not hardly. That was part of it. The money problems were bad enough, but what really killed our marriage was his... wandering eye. Vince always had someone in the choir who needed a "mentor." [pause] I'm sorry, that sounds bitter. But when you've caught your husband having "private vocal coaching sessions" with one too many pretty young things, you start to see patterns.

Joss: Vince was unfaithful?

Marianne: I won't smear his name, but Vince had a gift for making women feel special. And sometimes that gift got him in trouble. Would it surprise me if he'd gotten involved with the wrong man's wife? Not one bit. [pause] If you're looking for motives... Well, Vince had a way of making enemies without even trying. When I heard someone had run his car off the road... [voice breaks slightly] part of me wasn't surprised.

Joss: What do you mean?

Marianne: Vince lived his life like he was untouchable. Like his charm could get him out of any situation. But you can only push people so far before someone pushes back. [pause] I just... I never thought it would end like this. Whatever Vince did, my daughter didn't deserve to lose her father.

Joss: Before we end, I want to express my condolences about another tragedy striking your family before the holidays. Khalil Rogers better known as KJ. Was Vince a father figure to him?

Marianne: [long pause, voice softening] KJ... [another pause] Vince took a special interest in him. More like a big brother. That boy looked up to Vince so much. [voice becoming thick with emotion] Vince had a way of recognizing talent, and KJ... he had such a beautiful voice. Such promise cut short. At least he's with his mother now. Bless both of them.

Joss: Thank you for sharing with us, Marianne.

Marianne: Thank you for having me.

Joss: That was Marianne Hartman giving us a different perspective on Vince Hartman. Her interview raises new questions about Vince's personal and financial dealings in the weeks before his death. Were Vince's charm and financial troubles factors in his death?

Also, someone close to Marianne and Vince lost his life early last week. We'd like to make sure his case doesn't grow cold as well. If you have any information about Vince or KJ, call the CPD tip line.

I'm Joss Miller, the host of *Cold Justice* podcast.

Chapter 14
Bad Vibes

Tuesday, November 26 at 3:44 p.m.

Not surprised, but still a bit shook. Marianne's episode had the most downloads of all episodes. Period. I guess when the ex-wife finally spills the tea about her ex-husband that was one to tune into. I didn't want that type of podcast, but someone was angry enough to run Vince off the road. Marianne presented a multitude of reasons.

"I thought Fay didn't like for us to have our phone out all the time?" A nasally voice said from behind me.

I lifted my head. Fay always had new students from the local colleges working as baristas. They came and went, while I remained. It's one of the reasons why I was an assistant manager. But I wasn't going to throw that in the newest employee's face. She was so new I had to glance at her name tag.

Amber.

"You're right. I will get this customer coming in." I stuffed my phone in my apron. "Have you stocked the condiments yet?" Apparently the newbie needed something to do besides being in my business.

Amber grimaced and then went to the back. Her long blond ponytail swung as she walked.

"Joss, do you have a minute?"

A familiar voice asked from across the counter. I almost did a double take.

Sophia Carlson had walked in, but she was almost unrecognizable. Her hair was hastily pulled back, missing its usual shine. She wore no makeup and thick framed glasses.

I carefully inquired. "Sophia?"

"Yes." She peered down at her attire as if she didn't recognize herself. The cream colored cardigan she wore was cute, but the long t-shirt and leggings made it look like maybe she'd come from a workout. Except she wasn't wearing sneakers. I liked her Uggs boots, but it was not cold enough outside for them.

"Can I get you anything?"

Sophia squinted up at the menu above, even with the glasses on. "Sure, a caramel cappuccino is fine. I will be over here."

I watched her pace the café before sitting at a table in the middle. She pulled out the chair and faced the door.

I reached for the caramel syrup, adding three quick pumps into a warm cup before pulling a double shot of espresso. The rich aroma filled my nostrils as I watched the dark liquid stream over the caramel base. After pouring in the steamed milk, I added a drizzle of caramel. I walked the cup over to Sophia who sat twisting the strap of her bag.

"Here you go." I placed the cup in front of her.

Sophia jumped as if I'd startled her.

"Are you okay?"

She leaned forward and took a sip of the caramel cappuccino. "This is good. Um, I... I listened to your latest episode. The one with Marianne. I'm surprised she talked to you."

Something about her demeanor had my internal alarm bells ringing. "What did you think?"

Sophia's perfectly manicured nails were chipped today, one or two looked like they'd been bitten down. She absently drummed her fingers against the table. "Some of what she said—" She stopped abruptly, her eyes fixing on something through the front window. All the color drained from her face.

"Sophia?" I turned to look but didn't see anyone.

What or who was she seeing?

She stood up so quickly her chair scraped against the floor. "I shouldn't be here. I'm sorry." She gathered her purse with trembling hands. "Just... be careful, Joss. Please be careful."

"Wait!" I called after her, but she was already rushing toward the door. "What do you mean? And you forgot your caramel cappuccino."

The bell above the door chimed as she hurried out, leaving me staring after her with a knot forming in my stomach. I hurried over to the window to see what she'd seen.

Where did she go? What was she trying to say?

I turned my head to look in the other direction.

There was no sign of Sophia. I gazed at the street a few minutes.

She seemed genuinely surprised, even scared that Marianne did the interview on the podcast. I tried to recall some of the episode. Marianne had said a lot and appeared to be at peace after getting it off her chest.

I pulled out my phone to text Andre. He'd told me to let him know if anything strange happened, and this was weird.

> **Joss: Sophia Carlson just came to the café totally freaked out about the Marianne episode. She started to tell me something but something spooked her.**

Literally told me to "be careful" before bolting. She looked terrified.

I made my way back to the counter. Amber eyed me. I know I looked like I wasn't working, but I'd been employed at the café longer and closed up the café several days a week. And I arrived early in the morning to help Fay set up for the day. I didn't need the noob giving me a questioning eye.

I wanted to say something, but I smiled instead. "You're doing a great job."

I got an eyeroll from Amber.

That was fine. I had a feeling Amber wasn't going to last long here.

I needed to hear back from Andre. I peered down at my phone to find the annoying ellipses. At least he was responding. A few more agonizing seconds, then Andre's text appeared.

Andre: If Sophia was that spooked, there's a reason. Getting some strange coincidences between these hit and runs. Too early to confirm the connection, but my gut says something's off. Head straight home when the café closes. And call me when you arrive.

I looked at the clock. 4:00 p.m. I had another two hours to go.

Tuesday, November 26 at 5:56 p.m.

Fay emerged from her office as the afternoon rush died down. Amber had left thirty minutes before. Fay agreed the girl probably wouldn't make it to another shift. We split up the usual tasks for closing the café.

On my last trip back to the kitchen, Fay stopped me. "Something is wrong, isn't it? You have that wrinkle in your forehead like you're concentrating really hard on something. I heard the episode with Marianne. Did she say something?"

"No. Actually, Sophia Carlson came in earlier. But, Fay, I barely recognized her. Her hair was a mess, she looked scared to death, and then she ran out of here like someone was chasing her."

Fay's eyebrows shot up above her turquoise frames. "Sophia Carlson? Looking a hot mess?" She shook her head. "I've never seen that woman with a hair out of place."

"What do you know about her? Besides that she's married to Grant Carlson."

Fay wrinkled her nose. "Not much if I'm honest. I think she grew up going to another church, but when she married Grant, she started going to Greater Zion. She has a beautiful voice, a soprano, I'm talking able to hit notes like Mariah Carey beautiful. I think I heard that she went to Julliard, but I've never really heard if she did anything with her voice professionally."

"Do you know what she does? Do they have children?"

Fay shook her head. "No, they don't have children. I know she worked as a secretary at the church. But honestly, I'm not sure what else she does. Why are you asking all these questions? Any idea about what might have scared her off?"

I shook my head. "No. She disappeared so fast. Maybe Lily knows. They seemed to be good friends. I'm worried about her."

I whipped out my phone, scrolled to my messages and started typing.

> **Joss: Hey, have you seen or heard from Sophia today? She came by the café acting really strange.**

I started to slip my phone back in my apron, but it buzzed with a message.

"Wow, that was fast."

Fay looked at me. "Lily responded?"

I read the text.

> **Lily: No, haven't seen her. Hoping she would talk to you after hearing the interview with Marianne. Sophia and Vince were close. She knows things.**

I frowned. "What things could she know?"

Fay said thoughtfully, "Sophia was in the choir. I guess she knew Vince pretty well."

We both grabbed our bags and headed out the front. While Fay locked up, my phone buzzed again with another message.

> **Lily: Can you come over after work? There's something I need to talk to you about. Something that's been bugging me. I know you will understand.**

I stated out loud, "Uh-oh, Andre wanted me to head straight home."

Fay adjusted her glasses. "Where else were you thinking of going?"

We crossed the street together. "Lily asked me to come over. It should be fine, right?"

Fay tilted her head as if trying to process the idea. "The way Sophia ran out of here, maybe you should wait to visit Lily during the daytime."

One part of me wanted to head home. It had been a long day, but the other part of me was stuck on what was I missing. Maybe Lily had received some clarity around what Vince had been involved in. Of course if she did, she should be sharing that with the police, not me.

I sighed. "Lily lives with her mother. It should be fine to stop by."

Fay gave me a look as she climbed into her car. "You better let Andre know about the change of plans."

"I will." I pressed my key fob and settled inside my car. Locking the doors, I pulled out my phone and quickly typed a text message to Andre:

> Joss: Making a quick stop at Lily's. Then heading straight home.

The ellipses appeared immediately. I watched them bounce for a second before shoving my phone deep into my purse. Andre was probably typing out all the reasons this was a bad idea.

I looked over to see Fay observing me. The rule was we left the parking lot at the same time, me first. I cranked my engine and pulled out of the parking lot, heading in the opposite direction of home. My purse beside me buzzed persistently. Andre was probably alternating between texts and calls now.

I needed to get this over with. I'd set up location sharing on my phone after the incident this past summer. I was pretty comfortable with Andre knowing where to find me.

I might need him before the night was over.

Tuesday, November 26 at 7:13 p.m.

For a while, Fay drove behind me since I was going in her direction. She eventually turned off and I kind of missed having my big sister boss behind me. Now on my own, I realized I needed to remember the turnoff to Lily's house. I'd gone during the day last time. The drive to Lily's felt longer than usual.

Normally, my drive home was pretty quiet, not as many headlights. I wasn't sure why I was jumpy, but ever since Fay turned off, I kept looking in the rearview mirror. I should have been focusing on where I was heading. To help me focus, I turned off the music which was connected to my phone.

The silence didn't help.

One car stayed behind me for several blocks, and I found myself gripping the steering wheel.

Nobody is following you, girl.

But I couldn't help but wonder what happened that night when Vince's car shot off the road. Did he see the person behind him? Did they rush up on him with bright headlights blinding him?

My heartrate spiked when I realized I had to squint because I couldn't see. My first reaction was to smash the brake pedal. The car behind seemed to slow, probably wondering if the person in front of them forgot how to drive. With my heart still thundering in my chest, I recognized the street where Lily stayed with her mother.

I slowed, trying to recall the house number. Then I realized I couldn't see any house numbers and hoped I recognized the Foster's home. The flower beds in the front gave me my clue. I turned into the driveway and shut off the engine. I peered in my rearview mirror and watched a dark sedan drive by me.

Way to go with freaking out, Joss!

The porchlight was warm and inviting, but the temperature felt like it had dropped from the time I left the café, which wasn't more than fifteen minutes ago.

I rang the doorbell.

Like the first time, I visited, Evelyn opened the door. "Joss?"

"Hello, Mrs. Foster. Lily asked me to stop by."

She looked dubious. "Come on in. We're letting the heat out." Once I stepped inside, Evelyn peered around the doorway as if she expected someone else to be there with me. Satisfied, she closed the door.

"Come to the living room. Can I get you anything?"

"No, ma'am. I'm fine."

Lily's voice called down from above. "Mom, is that Joss?"

"Yes." Evelyn answered with a slight annoyance to her voice.

I hoped we weren't disturbing Lily's mother.

I quietly entered behind Evelyn into the living room, which appeared different in the soft glow of various lamps positioned around the room. Behind me, the pitter patter of footsteps hurried down the stairs.

Lily arrived looking out of breath. "Thank you for coming, Joss. I know you probably had a long day at work, but when you told me about Sophia, I thought we better talk."

Evelyn shook her head and grumbled as she passed her daughter. "You young people are always stirring up stuff."

Lily sat down in the same chair as before.

"Before we start, can you tell me why you chose Vince over Jake?"

Lily's face tightened. "Why do you need to know that?"

"I'm in love right now and when I see you with Jake, you remind me of how I feel with Andre."

Lily's face contorted into several emotions before landing on resolution. "I have had a year since Vince's death wondering what would have happened if we'd never gotten married." She sighed. "Jake and I had been together so long. When I turned thirty, it started to really hit me hard. I wanted marriage and children. We'd broken up and got back together so many times, but the last time, I was done waiting."

"And Vince?"

Lily twisted her wedding ring. It was the first time I noticed that she wore it. "Vince was a bit lost after he divorced Marianne. He needed to have a wife, I think. It helped with his image." Lily laughed harshly. "I took it as a joke when Valerie came to me saying her brother needed cheering up and I did too. I knew his reputation and Val is my girl, but I told her no way. Eventually, I went out with him. He was such a charmer. And I really did fall in love with him."

"You knew about his reputation and still fell for him?"

Lily cringed. "Like Marianne said on the episode, Vince had a way of making you feel special."

"Tell me about Sophia." I pressed. "What was her relationship with Vince really like?"

Lily pressed her lips together and stared at me for a few moments. With a resigned look on her face, she answered. "She was his star soprano. Everyone knew that. But..." She hesitated. "There was something about Marianne's interview that hit me square in the face. I think I spent so much time trying to keep people from bad-mouthing our relationship, that I often overlooked the root cause of all those rumors."

Lily wouldn't look at me. "You know when they told me where his accident was, the first thing that came to mind was what woman was he going to see. He was nowhere near his family's home.

"That's when it hit me. What was it Marianne said? Vince always had someone in the choir who needed a "mentor" or "private vocal coaching session."

I nodded, comprehension sinking in. "I think I understand why Sophia looked so terrified today. She was really surprised that Marianne decided to be interviewed. I think it was something Marianne said."

A car door slammed somewhere on the street. We both jumped.

Lily tilted her head. "Are you parked in the driveway?"

I nodded.

Then the doorbell rang as if someone was violently pushing the button.

I stared at Lily. "Are you expecting someone else?"

With wide eyes, Lily looked toward the door. "No."

Then the banging started.

Chapter 15

Chaos

Tuesday, November 26 at 7:13 p.m.

The doorbell's violent ringing gave way to thunderous pounding that shook the doorframe.

"Open this door!" A male voice roared from outside. "I know you're in there!"

Alarmed, I looked at Lily. "Is that who I think it is?"

She nodded. "He shouldn't be here. We got a restraining order." Above us, floorboards creaked as Evelyn's footsteps moved across the second floor.

The banging continued. "Please, I need to talk to you."

I stood to my feet. "You should call the police."

We heard Evelyn descending the stairs, muttering, "This foolishness has got to stop."

"Mom, no!" Lily jumped up. "Just call the police!"

"I've had enough of this nonsense," Evelyn's voice carried from the foyer. "I'm putting an end to it tonight."

The door lock clicked.

BANG!

Lily screamed. I clutched my chest as my heart leaped in fright.

Was that a gunshot?

A man's agonized scream filled the air. "You crazy woman! You shot me!"

Lily rushed past me into the foyer. "Mom! Put the gun down!"

My legs finally remembered how to move. I followed Lily to find Terrell sprawled on the front porch, clutching his leg. Blood seeped between his fingers. Evelyn stood in the doorway, a small revolver steady in her hands.

"I have every right to protect my home," Evelyn declared, her voice ice-cold. "I warned you to stay away from my house. Leave my daughter alone. Your family has done enough."

"Mom, please," Lily begged. "Put the gun down."

My hands shook as I pulled out my phone and dialed 911. "Yes, we need an ambulance at 742 Maple Street. A man's been ... shot." I stumbled with my words as I caught sight of the blood pooling on Terrell's pants. My limited first aid training kicked in. We needed to stop the bleeding.

"Lily, we need something to stop this bleeding," I called out, trying to keep my voice steady. "A towel, anything."

Lily touched her mother's arm gently. "Mom, he's hurt. Let me get a towel. Please put the gun down – he's not going anywhere like this."

Evelyn's grip on the revolver loosened slightly, but her eyes remained fixed on Terrell. "He shouldn't have come here threatening us. I'm tired of it."

Terrell yelled, "I wasn't going to do anything. I'm not the one you should be afraid of."

Lily disappeared into the house, returning moments later with a large towel. I took it from her, then approached Terrell slowly, my heart hammering. Suppose he tried to grab me or something. "I can help you wrap this around your leg, okay?"

Terrell writhed in pain on the porch, his face contorted. "Ju st... just help me!"

"What were you doing here?" I asked, cautiously holding out the towel. "Were you planning to hurt someone?"

"Me? Hurt someone?" He laughed bitterly through his pain. "I'm the one who got shot! I was trying to help!"

Remembering what I heard a few minutes ago, I asked. "Help with what? Who should we be afraid of?" I managed to get the towel wrapped around his calf and then tied it to make a tourniquet.

Terrell gritted his face in pain, but he didn't answer.

I had a feeling I already knew.

The pieces had started to come together for me.

A flash of red and blue lights sped down the street. I stepped away from Terrell as an ambulance pulled in front of the house. As I heard car doors slamming, I peered around the doorway thinking of what Terrell had stated.

I'm not the one you should be afraid of.

Tuesday, November 26 at 7:37 p.m.

Andre pulled me away from the chaos on the porch where paramedics were now tending to Terrell. A deputy was taking Evelyn's statement, the revolver safely secured in an evidence bag.

"Grant Carlson," I said before Andre could speak. "That's who Terrell came to warn us about, isn't it?"

Andre's jaw tightened. "How did you figure that out?"

"Marianne talked about how Vince mentored or had special private vocal sessions, and these were mainly with women. I think one of those women was Sophia. She always seemed to have this fondness for Vince... like they had a special relationship."

Andre looked at me his face resigned. "Keep going. Sounds like you've given this a lot of thought, Detective Miller."

I rolled my eyes. "Anyhow, I bet if you look back at the road where Vince had his accident, it was near the Carlson's house. Am I right?"

Andre's eyes widened slightly. "You think Vince died due to jealousy?"

I crossed my arms. "It's a good motive. Jealous husband runs lover off the road. Sophia knew something. She was scared."

"Well, Grant's already in custody. We got him about an hour ago." Andre said, rubbing his forehead. "But he's not there for Vince's murder."

"No?" I asked confused.

"I'm working KJ's murder." Andre reminded, as he stuffed his hands into his pants pockets. "I started looking into why we couldn't trace the car from the hit-and-run. Someone knew how to make the vehicle disappear."

I snapped my finger. "Someone with access to cars. Did you suspect Terrell?"

"Yeah, after that scene at the dealership," Andre said. "Something felt off about how he lost his cool that day. It was almost like he was nervous too."

"So what changed?"

"Started digging into Terrell's background. Man's got a clean record except for some parking tickets. But knowing KJ also worked at Carlson Auto, that's when things got interesting." Andre lowered his voice. "Got an anonymous tip about Grant running luxury cars through illegal channels. High-end vehicles disappearing and reappearing with clean papers."

"And you think that's why KJ died? Because he knew about the car scheme?"

"KJ was in the perfect position to spot irregularities in the paperwork."

I glanced back at the porch where Terrell was being loaded into the ambulance. "Why did he come here tonight?"

Andre sighed. "We learned Grant helped Terrell out of some serious debts. Kept him under his thumb that way. We think

Terrell suspected Grant for his brother's so-called accident, but felt trapped. When he heard about your podcast…"

"He was trying to warn us off," I finished. "To keep us from digging too far."

"I have a feeling Terrell's been terrified of Grant's retaliation if the truth came out. The scene at the dealership. That was a man on the verge of snapping, desperate to get out from under Grant's control."

I watched as Lily comforted her mother, who still looked shaken but defiant.

"So what happens now?"

Andre looked at me. "You need to head straight home like you agreed to do earlier."

I grimaced. "Ah, come on. I gave you more reasons to put Grant behind bars, helped you wrap-up Vince's case."

Andre held up his hand. "Not yet. We still need to gather evidence. Preferably, we need a confession from Grant."

"He might as well confess. You already got him for the fraud, theft and KJ's murder."

I suddenly felt really exhausted. "I'm going to get in my car. Are you sure I can go?"

Andre nodded. "I got you."

He walked me over and closed the door after I climbed inside.

My phone buzzed as I put the key in the ignition. After everything that happened, I almost ignored it. But when I glanced at the screen, my mouth fell open.

"What's wrong?" Andre knocked on the window.

I slid the window down and held up my phone to show him Nate's text:

> **Nate: "I saw your message about KJ. Man, he was a good guy. Thanks for letting me know, sis."**

"Only a week later." I muttered. "The Millers are an interesting bunch."

"Yeah, wait until you meet the Baez clan at Thanksgiving in a few days," Andre chuckled. "I would say we're a lot louder and more drama-filled."

"Thanksgiving?" My eyes widened. With everything going on, I'd completely forgotten about the holiday. "That's ..."

"Thursday," he confirmed with a grin. "Don't tell me you forgot you agreed to meet my family?"

I groaned and let my head fall back against the headrest.

Andre squeezed my shoulder. "Drive safe. I'll be right behind you."

I nodded, too tired to even worry about meeting his family anymore. One crisis at a time was all I could handle right now.

Epilogue
Thanksgiving Day

I observed the organized chaos unfolding in Andre's kitchen. My mother and Andre's mother, Gloria, chatted as they prepared a feast. Andre had started the Mojo turkey, a recipe he had to explain to me last night as he created the marinating sauce with citrus, garlic, oregano and olive oil. Once his mother had approved Andre's turkey, he was booted out of his own kitchen. With his mother, my mother, Louise and his three sisters in the fray, he seemed fine keeping a low profile as the only adult male.

I had no cooking skills, so I was happy to keep him company in the living room along with his nieces and nephews. Hard to believe the podcast episodes had brought so much attention to Vince Hartman. Now the traditional news media was picking up on the demise of Carlson Auto or at least the current owner. It sounded like the woman we met, Cindy, Grant's older sister would take the helm. My heart went out to her. Given all the recent press, attempting to keep the family business alive despite the controversy of her brother's fraudulent activities might prove to be a lot.

I was sure the Carlson's Thanksgiving would not be a peaceful one.

In the meantime, I loved smelling all the mingling aromas of traditional Southern Thanksgiving dishes like my mother's greens and macaroni and cheese, Louise's buttermilk biscuits and the Cuban specialties that Gloria brought to the table. I'd always known Andre had Latino roots from his father's side. Apparently to entice Andre's dad, his mother learned how to cook all his dad's favorite recipes. For the first time, I would taste Arroz Congri, Cuban rice and black beans and Plátanos Maduros, sweet fried plantains.

Andre's sisters—Carmen, Sofia, and Maria—true to Andre's warning, peppered me with questions from the moment they arrived. However, their genuine warmth and infectious laughter made it impossible to feel anxious. I imagined they wouldn't be too bad as sisters-in-law if that day ever arrived.

I noticed Andre checking his phone again—something he'd been doing all morning. He kept glancing at the door too, and

I couldn't shake the feeling he was waiting for something. Or someone.

The doorbell rang, and Andre practically jumped to answer it. I followed him, curious about his unusual behavior.

When the door opened, I froze.

Standing there was my brother Nate.

"Surprise, little sis," he grinned, opening his arms.

I launched myself at him. "How... what...?"

"Your boyfriend here can be pretty persuasive," Nate said, nodding at Andre. "He tracked me down, introduced himself and suggested I might want to spend Thanksgiving with my family."

I turned to Andre, who was watching us with a satisfied smile. "You did this?"

I stepped back as my mother squeezed her son. My brother had played football and was always a big guy. His early thirties looked good on him. He'd kept his shape, and now sported a full beard.

Louise stood back and smiled. Nate didn't come home that often, so she hadn't gotten to know him. I hoped that would change. We all needed family.

I placed my arms around Andre's waist. "Thank you for doing this."

"I know how much you missed him," Andre shrugged. "And I figured if my whole family was going to be here, yours should be too."

Later, as we all settled around Andre's expanded dining room table, Nate said, "I've been keeping up with your podcast."

"You have?" I raised an eyebrow.

"You thought I wouldn't pay attention to my little sister's interest in true crime," Nate chuckled. "From your episodes, Sugar Creek sounds a lot more exciting than I remember."

"Well, maybe you will visit more often." I said.

Nate and Andre exchanged a look.

"What's going on?"

Nate shook his head. "I'll tell you later. I will be in Sugar Creek for a few days. In the meantime, I'm going to enjoy this meal. It's been awhile since I've had home cooking like this."

It was good to have my brother here. Hopefully, he would be home for Christmas too. I couldn't help but smile at how perfectly everything had come together. My family and Andre's, blending naturally. Even Louise and Clarice chatted among themselves without the tension that usually hung between them.

Andre caught my eye and winked.

I blushed, feeling happy and quite full too.

For that, I was truly thankful.

Author's Note

I want to give a special thanks to the readers who have embraced the Joss Miller Mysteries. When I decided to do a spin-off of the Eugeena Patterson Mysteries with a younger amateur sleuth, I only planned for a three book series. After reading the reviews and feedback, I'm very excited about continuing this series and already have plans for three more books. I enjoy the podcast format which is very different from my other series and look forward to Joss not only growing as a podcaster, but watching her relationship grow with Detective Andre Baez as well. Who knows wedding bells may be in a future book.

I felt compelled to introduce Andre's family and finally bring in an appearance for Nate Miller, Joss's often absent older brother. Hopefully, you didn't skip the epilogue because that exchange between Andre and Nate was very telling of what's to come in the fourth book in the series, *Steamy Espresso Secrets*. Look for this book sometime toward the end of 2025.

And I'm thinking it might be awesome to have a crossover book between Ms. Eugeena and Joss. Email me on my website or send me a direct message on my social media about your thoughts.

I want to thank my longtime editor, Felicia Murrell, for always pushing me to keep an open mind and polishing up my writing to deliver a clean read.

Special thanks to my mother and sister who I'm always going on and on about these characters in my head.

Whenever you get to read this book, I wish you joy not only during the holiday season, but all year-round.

About the Author

Tyora Moody is the author of **Soul-Searching Mysteries,** which includes **cozy mystery, women sleuth mystery,** and **romantic suspense** under the Christian Fiction genre. Her books include the Eugeena Patterson Mysteries, Joss Miller Mysteries, Serena Manchester Mysteries, Reed Family Mysteries, and the Victory Gospel Mysteries.

When Tyora isn't working for a literary client, she's either loving on her cats, listening to an audiobook or podcast, binge-watching crime shows or Marvel movies, and of course, thinking about the next book.

To contact Tyora about reviewing her books or book club discussions, visit her online at TyoraMoody.com.

Join her newsletter at https://tyoramoody.substack.com/

Tyora Moody's Books

Eugeena Patterson Mysteries

Deep Fried Trouble, #1

Oven Baked Secrets, #2

Lemon Filled Disaster, #3

A Simmering Dilemma, #4

An Unsavory Mess, #5

A Spicy Predicament, #6

Marinated Conditions, #7

Eugeena Patterson Family Shorts

Shattered Dreams, #1

A Blended Family Christmas, #2

Falling in Love... Again!, #3

TYORA MOODY

Joss Miller Mysteries
Double Mocha Blues, #1
A Latte Mayhem, #2
Mint-Flavored Trouble, #3

Serena Manchester Mysteries
Hostile Eyewitness, prequel
Bittersweet Motives, #1
Dangerous Confessions, #2
Waning Innocence, #3
Presumed Guilty, #4
Shifting Blame, #5

Lowcountry Secrets (Romantic Suspense)
The Homecoming, #1

Reed Family Mysteries
Broken Heart, #1
Troubled Heart, #2
Relentless Heart, #3
With All My Heart, #3.5
Faithful Heart, #4
Wounded Heart, #5

Victory Gospel Series (Mysteries)
When Rain Falls, #1
When Memories Fade, #2
When Perfection Fails, #3

Victory Gospel Shorts (Sweet Romance)
The Replacement Date, #1
Southern Delights, #2
When Love Finds Me, #3
Nobody's Replacement, #4
A Southern Delights Christmas, #5
Holding on to Love, #6